PASSPORT TO LIFE CITY

Books authored

PASSPORT TO LIFE CITY
THE SOCIAL CONSCIENCE OF THE EVANGELICAL
NOT ME, GOD
MAGNIFICENT PROMISE
OPEN YOUR BIBLE
CRUSADE AT THE GOLDEN GATE

Edited

THE QUIET CORNER
SPIRITUAL AWAKENING

PASSPORT

A Modern Pilgrim's Progress

Harper & Row, Publishers

TO LIFE CITY

by *SHERWOOD ELIOT WIRT*

1817

New York, Evanston, and London

Grateful acknowledgment is made to the publishers for permission to quote portions of the following songs: "Nothing Is Impossible," by Eugene L. Clark, © 1966 The Good News Broadcasting Association, Inc., Lincoln, Neb.; "His Name Is Wonderful," by Audrey Mieir, © 1959 Manna Music, Inc., Hollywood, Calif.; and "Turn It Over to Jesus," by Ray Hildebrand of the Fellowship of Christian Athletes, © 1968 Word Records Inc., Waco, Tex.

FIRST EDITION

LIBRARY OF CONGRESS CATALOG CARD NUMBER: 70-85041

For Billy and Ruth Graham

Preface

WHILE giving an address at Church House, London, in connection with the British edition of *Decision* magazine, I mentioned that I was preparing for publication a twentieth-century adaptation of John Bunyan's masterwork, *The Pilgrim's Progress.* Shortly thereafter a letter appeared in a Christian newspaper, deploring the whole idea and suggesting that I might better leave Bunyan alone and stick to my own experience of God. It was a word spoken in season and I took it to heart. The preacher of Bedford has never needed people like me to explain or interpret him. His genius speaks for itself.

The letter, however, did manage to bypass the cultural dilemma of the evangelical Christian today which caused me to undertake the present project. Just as many European Christians love and admire their ancient churches, but would prefer something more comfortable in which to worship, so many lovers of Christian literature are loyal to the writings of Bunyan, Milton, Donne and other classic evangelicals of the past—to say nothing of the King James Bible itself—but are finding it increasingly difficult to understand them.

For well over two hundred years *The Pilgrim's Progress* was the best-known book (after the Bible) in the English language. It was translated into scores and even hundreds of other tongues. The work is an allegory of the soul's journey in quest of God, all the more amazing because composed by a relatively uneducated man. Bunyan's mastery of the English language was acquired through reading the Bible and a few other spiritual volumes, such as Foxe's *Book of Martyrs*. The *Oxford Dictionary of the Christian Church* says of Bunyan's most famous work, "Its unrivalled place in the world's literature rests on its artless directness, its imaginative power, the homeliness and rusticity of its method and its plainness of style, which give it universal appeal, even to the most simple minded." The closer one studies the work, the more one is impressed by the author's craftsmanship, by the movement of his story line, by his use of Scripture and by his gifts of characterization and imagery.

Yet there are few today who care to take such a close look. Lovers of Bunyan, classicists and Christian antiquarians, along with thousands of everyday Christians, still read *Pilgrim's Progress* and profit from it; but humanity's millions are passing it by. No longer does it hold a place of unquestioned honor in the English-speaking Christian home. Many new Christians have never heard of it.

My story is not an attempt to "update" the Bedford tinker or to make a latter-day bid for a piece of his reputation. One does not set out to climb Mount Everest in sneakers! With such equipment as the Lord has given me, I have written a modern parable to show, if possible, what it means to search for the living God in our generation. How far this tale depends on the framework of *Pilgrim's Progress,* each reader must decide for himself. I wish to make it clear that John Bunyan is not responsible for the ideas or opinions expressed in *Passport to Life City.* Yet it will be more than obvious that without Bunyan's masterpiece the present work could not have taken shape. A list of characters and places at the end of the book serves to relate the nomenclature of the two tales.

I would like to thank my wife Winola and my son Alexander, and many fellow employees of The Billy Graham Evangelistic Association, for kindly reading and listening to these chapters and for making numerous valuable suggestions. The editors at Harper & Row have been most helpful. Particularly do I thank Miss Ethel Beckstrom, editorial assistant on the staff of *Decision,* who prepared the typescript and whose sustained enthusiasm and critical encouragement made it possible for the manuscript to be completed in the midst of journalistic duties.

Whatever its deficiencies, the aim of *Passport to Life City* is identical with that of *Pilgrim's Progress*: to help men and women find their way, by God's own directions, into the everlasting joy of his Kingdom of love in Christ Jesus.

Now put yourself behind the wheel—as I did—and take off!

S.E.W.

Begun at Forest Home, California, July 1968
Finished at Minneapolis, Minnesota, January 1969

PASSPORT TO LIFE CITY

Chapter 1

FIRST there was the pain. It had come without warning one evening as a burning sensation between his shoulder blades. At the time Chris Anders was sitting quietly at home, reading (of all things) the New Testament. Within a few days a hard, preoccupying knot of soreness had developed on his upper spine.

Then there was the state of the world. It was as if someone had sat on the panic button. Peking radio broadcasts were hourly screaming fresh warnings of imminent thermonuclear disaster. Congress had been called into special session. It seemed to Chris that this was it.

Then there was the almost hopeless situation at home. As he buttoned his shirt that Saturday morning, he tried once again to analyze what had happened to his family, and gave up. Staring into the mirror, Chris realized that the corners of his mouth had flattened into something bleak, and his nostrils had turned white. He slipped into his jacket and descended the narrow carpeted staircase. As he passed the living room he looked in on his younger sons, Jeffrey and Dana, gnawing pretzels in front of the television set. They were, it appeared, well locked into the vagaries of a space-monster program.

He paused a moment as if to speak, then changed his mind, went to the front closet and took out a topcoat. Mentally he checked over the rest of the family. Jerry? He had been invited to go surfing over the weekend. There had been a row about it, during which the generation gap had widened by a decade or so. Dean? Trouble there, too; he was going to an SDS rally at the municipal park. Chris had tried to put his foot down, and terrible words had been spoken.

At the front door he heard the sound of water running outside; that would be Eileen and her shrubs. He noticed the shine on his knuckles as he turned the knob and stepped out on the little front porch. The screen door banged; he saw Eileen turn, drop the hose, wipe her hands on her slacks, and approach him.

"So," she said.

"Yup."

"Did the boys see you?"

"Nope."

"I have the privilege of telling them, is that it?"

"Ee-yup."

Eileen reached into her pocket for her cigarettes. "For nineteen years every rotten job in this house has been dropped into my lap. Now this."

"Would you believe it if I told you that I invited each one of the boys individually to come on a trip with me, and they all turned me down? Jerry and Dean as much as told me we had nothing to say to each other. The young ones didn't want to miss their programs."

"I believe it."

"I even tried to talk to them again last night—"

"In the middle of a ball game. What did you expect? You spend your life on the road selling computers, then come home to children who hardly know you and want them to act like little tin soldiers."

Chris bit his lip. "I don't know what's happened to this house. It used to be great around here until a couple of years ago. Then all of a sudden things just fell apart."

"You don't know what happened? You want me to tell you?"

Chris ignored her and looked over at his new yellow Mustang, the one status symbol that had got through to his heart. "I know," he said slowly, "that nothing I ask people to do around here ever gets done. Nothing. Look at that car in the driveway. Mud smeared all over it. That's the story of my life. I asked Jerry to wash it, but would he do it? I asked you to iron my shirts and sew a button on my topcoat and clear out that upstairs closet. I asked if we could have Sally and Tom over last night. What do I get? More water on the shrubs."

"Really, you're being rather petty, aren't you?" Eileen snapped back. "Let me remind you of a thing or two that might explain what's happened, or hasn't happened. Like last Sunday night. . . ."

Chris reached inside the screen door and brought out a set of matching luggage. "Skip it," he said. "Go tell it to your marriage counselor. He'll mix you a drink and put his hand on your knee and inform you intelligently what a lemon you've got."

"Don't talk about him that way. You can't blame him."

"No, I'll just blame me. It's simpler. The reason you moved out of my room and decided not to be a wife to me any more is that I'm me."

"Chris, it's not my fault that you've let your life get to be such a mess. The more computers you sell, the worse things seem to be around here. No woman can stand the kind of treatment you've been giving me. I've done some wrong things, but—"

"Oh, let's not get coy—"

"What's the use! Won't you ever grow up?"

He tossed his luggage into the trunk of the Mustang and slammed the lid, wincing as he straightened up. The pain in his back was getting fierce. "If I do grow up," he said, "I'll write." He patted the newspaper in his pocket. "Hear about the war we're in?"

"The radio was on while I was trying to sleep. But I'm a little more concerned about the war in this household. Do you realize what you're doing to me? Just what do you think I'm going to tell the boys? And what do I use for money to feed them?"

"It's all worked out in the envelope I left upstairs on the bed. Tom knows the setup. He was coming with me until he changed his mind. I asked him to look after you and the kids. You can check with him about details."

"Does this mean you're walking out for good?"

"Maybe—— Maybe not. Strange as it may seem, maybe what I'm trying to do is salvage this marriage. Go away for a while and give you a chance to see what it's like without having old Anders around. Give those foul-mouthed kids a little shock treatment, too. Maybe they'll begin to appreciate their father and decide to shape up. Maybe I can find somebody who'll know what's wrong with my back. Doc Fletcher's certainly a washout."

"You won't solve your problems, Chris, by running away from them."

"Oh, I left you pretty well fixed," he said by way of answer. "You can hire a lawyer if you want. He'll promise you a real nice settlement. I've made top salesman in the district for eight months straight, so I should be fair game."

Eileen sat down on the front step. "Congratulations," she said. "What do I say when people start calling up from the office?"

"You can tell them anything you like. I arranged for a leave. Say I've been brainwashed by some religious nut." Chris slipped painfully into the leather bucket seat. "The girls at the garden club won't have to be told anything," he added. "When they hear I've split they'll just say, 'Poor old Chris, going through another of his phases.'"

"I'll say nothing of the kind. If anyone asks I'll simply tell them that you walked out on your obligations. You couldn't stand the sight of what you'd created, so you abandoned it."

"Fair enough," said Chris, turning the key in the ignition.

Eileen got to her feet. "Where do you think you're going?" she asked acidly.

"Who knows?" he said. "We've looked for help in all the usual places. Now I'm going to start looking in some of the unusual places. Want to come along?"

"You're being funny."

Chris backed the little car along the concrete driveway into the street. As he pulled ahead he took another look at his wife. She was standing by the irises, hose in hand, cigarette in mouth. There was a brief, inscrutable exchange of glances. As he rounded the corner he saw her carrying the hose toward a peony bush, adjusting the spray.

Chapter 2

ONCE on the open freeway, Chris gave the Mustang its head. It shot past two or three interchanges before he nosed it into a roadside rest area next to a barley field. He rolled past the picnic tables to a quiet spot and turned the key. Now all was silent except for the muffled hum of traffic in the distance. He sat completely still for a while and stared at a starling that was eyeing him from a nearby fencepost. There was, he decided, something menacing about that bird. When if flew off it came directly over the Mustang.

Chris turned on the radio and caught the start of a newscast: ". . . threatened to attack all of North America with fifty nuclear-tipped ICBM's unless the United States guarantees within forty-eight hours to withdraw the Seventh Fleet from the Taiwan perimeter. The President is expected to issue a statement from the White House this morning rejecting the latest demand. . . ." He tuned out the station.

So we may have only a few hours to live Well I've come to my senses at last It took forty-three years but I know what I want

In the short time left I'm going to start looking for God Don't know what this means Not sure anyone else does but what I read in the Bible sure rang a bell Maybe if I could even get a little while to think without anything else on my mind without having to fight somebody Haven't been to church Don't care to be told my life is a mess Been dragged to psychologists and family clinics till I feel like a piece of salami under a microscope This inflammation between my shoulder blades is driving me right over the edge Looks like the kid business turned out sour for us I wonder how they fix those monoxide hose things in the car No I'm going to give God a chance first If I only knew somebody. . . .

A black Chevelle pulled into the rest area, and Chris saw through his rearview mirror that the driver had got out and was coming toward him. He began to roll up the window, but there was something about the way the man approached with hand extended that made him pause—with three inches to go.

"It's all right," said the stranger. He was about thirty-five with a tanned, friendly face.

"Lost your way?" asked Chris.

"No——thanks. I just saw you parked here, and since I'm taking polls at random I thought I'd stop."

"What kind of polls?"

"Just information about people, actually. Nothing personal. Here's my card. Mind if I ask you a few questions?" He took a large envelope from his pocket.

"I suppose you heard the news this morning," said Chris.

"Yes, I did." No emotion showed on his face. Chris rolled the window back down.

"Go ahead."

"Well, here's a list of people, and I would say that most of them are known to you. You're supposed to help me grade them from one to five. One means that you don't think much of them. You don't feel they're important, and they don't carry much weight as far as you're concerned. Five means they are very important to you. And you can pick any number in between. Get it?"

"I guess so."

"OK. On this basis, how would you rate the Green Bay Packers?"

"One."

"Johnny Carson."

"Two and a half."

"Charlie Brown."

"Four."

"Dr. Christiaan Barnard."

"Oh—two. Who wants to live that badly?"

"Leonard Bernstein."

"One."

"Phyllis Diller."

"Zero."

"Maharishi Mahesh."

"Zero."

"Mohammed Ali."

"You mean Cassius? Minus one."

"Che Guevara."

"Minus one."

"Mao Tse-tung."

"Ask me that one tomorrow."

"Jesus of Nazareth."

Chris sucked his breath through his teeth and thought for

a long moment. He glanced at the card in his hand. It read E. VAN GELST, RELIGIOUS CONSULTANT. There was no address. "Five," he said at last.

The man smiled and tucked the envelope back in his coat pocket. "I didn't catch your name," he said.

"Anders. I sell computers—or I used to. Yours is van—"

"Ernie van Gelst."

"Tell me, is this quiz thing a gimmick? Do you use it to get people to talk about religion?"

"Sometimes."

"Well, now. You say your name's Ernie?"

"It is to you."

"Well, I'm in a kind of—the fact is, I just left—I mean, when I heard the network tell about—what do you do when the world seems to be falling apart, Ernie? Your own world too. How do you connect to something that makes sense?"

"It sounds to me as if you have been reading the Bible."

"Some."

"Got troubles at home?"

"Plenty. And then this thing on my—"

A screech of brakes on the freeway made them turn their heads. A Pontiac had pulled onto the shoulder; the driver had evidently spotted them and was backing up to enter the turnoff to the rest area. Van Gelst turned back and patted Chris on the arm. "Anders," he said, "do you see that radio tower on the hill, with the red light blinking?"

"What about it?"

"That's the transmitter, of course. You head for it. It's right on the main county road, and there's a small building connected to it. After you ring the bell, show the engineer this card. He'll answer your questions. Apparently these men want to talk to you, and I've got some more stops to make down the road before lunch. Don't forget, now. God in your heart!"

And he was in his car and gone, just as a Bonneville drew alongside the Mustang. Chris recognized the driver as O. B. Stennett, an occasional golfing partner who lived across the street from him. He and the man with him were wearing sport shirts. They were evidently ready for a Saturday morning of eighteen holes.

"I told Warren I bet anything that was your Mustang," said O. B., whose closely cropped head protruded from his shoulders like a bullet. "Meet Warren Clay—he works in our department." There was a pause. "Like to make it a threesome?" he asked after a moment.

Chris shook his head. "I didn't bring my clubs. You guys are playing it smart. Hear the news?"

"Yup," said O. B. There was silence. O. B. switched on a music station. "Eileen was over," he said.

Chris nodded.

"Anything we can do to help?"

"Not a thing."

"You going somewhere?"
back, for one thing."

"Got a lead. I've got to get rid of this business in my
"What's the matter with Doc Fletcher?"

"Hasn't helped."

"OK." Stennett looked into his rearview mirror. "You know what you're doing—I guess."

"Wait a minute," said Clay, reaching for the door handle.

He jumped out and came over to the Mustang. "Who was that fellow you were talking to a minute ago? The one who drove off?"

"Name's van Gelst, I think," said Chris.

"That's the guy. I ran into him a couple of weeks ago. He's interesting."

"Yes, he is."

"Did he say something about that transmitter up there?"

"As a matter of fact, he did."

"That where you're going now?"

"Might."

"Do you mind company?"

"Get in."

Clay turned back to the other car and began lifting his clubs out of the back seat.

"What are you trying to pull, you silly ass?" roared O. B.

"I didn't really feel like playing anyway," said Clay.

"He can't help you! Don't you know that? This guy's a mental case. Been one for months. His wife's been telling us all about him."

Clay paused, waiting for Chris to unlock the door.

"We're signed up to tee off in fifteen minutes," yelled O. B.

"Sorry about that," said Clay. "Give my regrets to the starter. Take care, now."

O. B. reached over, grabbed the door handle of the Bonneville and slammed it shut. "Whatever it is you're looking for," he said, "I hope you fall in." He started up, swung his car in front of Chris' Ford and stopped. "I suppose you call this religion," he said. "Ditch your wife and kids, run around telling the world the sky's going to fall, get your friends fouled up and take off on a wild goose chase. All because you've got a pain in your shoulder. I'll tell you where you give me a pain. I'll see you both in—"

He drove off with squealing tires, leaving Chris and Warren Clay in a cloud of exhaust fumes. They started up and moved down the freeway at a more moderate speed, watching the signs for a turnoff that would lead toward the transmitter away in the distance. Before long they came to an interchange that peeled off in the right direction. By this time they were engaged in a frank reappraisal of the prospects that lay ahead of them and an evaluation of the good faith of Ernie van Gelst; and neither paid attention when a sign flashed past them reading WRONG WAY. DO NOT ENTER. Almost before they knew it the car was lurching over a pitted gravel stretch that led down toward a creekbed. A sign appeared on the right saying simply DANGER. Rounding a bend, they found to their dismay that the road disappeared into the waters of what seemed a wide, shallow, muddy slough.

"Shall we try it?" asked Chris.

"You're the boss," said Warren.

"I don't think we have anything to worry about," Chris decided. "That flash flood last night must have ripped out the old bridge after the work crews took off for the weekend. 'Tisn't deep, really. And these eight cylinders will take us through just about anything." With that he put the stick into low and moved ahead. The little Ford zipped confidently into the current, which turned out to be somewhat stronger and faster than expected. Two-thirds of the way across, the Mustang struck a low spot with the right front wheel and the water came up partially over the hood. A cloud of steam arose, accompanied by loud hissing and coughing noises. Chris rocked the car back and forth, but as it settled the gears became less responsive to his touch. The engine stalled, and he began furiously working the starter button. Though the flywheel made a few valiant efforts, it became apparent that the cylinders were hopelessly submerged.

"Your plugs are wet," said Clay. "It's a waste of time."

"I think we can start it," said Chris. He got out, sloshed to the front of the car, lifted the hood and watched the dirty water pouring through the motor.

"Don't be ridiculous," said Clay. "It's not going to start. Are you sure you knew where you were going when you turned off?"

"Reasonably sure."

"Any idea where we are now?"

"Frankly, no. I never took this road before."

Clay sighed. "How you'll get out of this, Anders, I don't know, but I think I've been had. Right now I wish I was on that course with O. B." He took off his shoes and socks and began rolling up his trousers.

"Where are you thinking of going?" asked Chris.

"I'm not sure," said Clay, "except that it's the opposite direction from yours. I leave you all your happy prospects, brother. I'm going to learn to live with my pains."

"Wait, Warren," said Chris. "This is supposed to be a main road. Someone will be coming along to help us."

"Anders," said Clay, putting his feet distastefully into the chocolate-colored water, "this kid is not waiting for anybody." He waded back to where the car had entered the stream, put on his shoes and disappeared.

For the first time the real import of what had happened came home to Chris. He got back in the car and sat for a few moments in dismal contemplation, while the water gurgled through the floorboards. He felt very alone and depressed. It was obvious that his attempt to escape from Doomsdale had turned into a fiasco.

What a stupid thing to do to a good car Anders old son This was a fizzle When Clay tells Stennett about this Ahh phooey on Stennett and phooey on Clay and phooey on this creek What a cotton-pickin' mess I'm sick to death of trying any more What were those lines "I am poured out like water and all my bones are out of joint my heart is like wax it is melted within my breast" How about that After twenty years that Bible lit course keeps coming back to me Well why not That's where I met Eileen She used to help me out of jams like this Isn't there some way to stop this pain besides sticking my head in a waterhole and keeping it there . . . .

Chris now faced the problem of extricating himself and his vehicle. As he looked around he saw bits of garbage floating past and realized that the stream was polluted with open sewage. Climbing out, he took a towrope from the trunk and tried to secure it to the front end of the car. When he reached for the axle he floundered into the same hole that had trapped his Ford. The disgusting water rose almost to his neck and swirled so threateningly that he expected at any moment to be engulfed. His confidence in van Gelst began to ebb. He doubted whether he would ever find relief from the pain, or that the transmitter engineer or anyone else could help him. The Mustang was stuck, and he did not know where to turn.

Something white came up out of the water and floated away. It was the newspaper from his pocket; as he watched it go he could still see a part of the giant headline, CHINA THREAT. He struggled to secure the lashing as stones rolled over his feet. The nauseating sewer smell almost overpowered him; and the thought went through his mind that not just he, Chris Anders, but the whole world was in that hole, struggling for survival and up to its neck in the muck of its endless predicaments.

A sudden sweep of current tore his hand from the fender to which he clung. Now he held only to the rope and was carried toward the center of the stream. At this moment he heard faintly through plugged ears a voice calling from the nearer shore, and turning his head with an effort, saw that a jeep had appeared, and that a black highway worker with a metal hat and red flagman's shirt was getting out of it.

"Don't try to move," he shouted. "I'll throw you a line."

Dimly, Chris was aware of the accuracy with which the man pitched the coiled rope within arm's reach. He seized it and quickly tied it to his own rope. Then he followed it ashore, stumbling and retching until he fell on the bank. For the next twenty minutes he lay doubled up, convulsively gasping for breath, while the road worker, after trying to make him comfortable, maneuvered his jeep to bring the disabled vehicle ashore. At last the dirty, dripping little car emerged on the road, and after blocking its wheels the man came over to Chris as he sat against a tree, wringing out his socks.

"My name's Anders," Chris nodded weakly. "Thanks a lot. You shouldn't have bothered."

"Upman." They made a motion to shake hands, and laughed. "What did you do, miss the road?"

"No," said Chris, "I was actually on the road heading for the transmitter. I saw the bridge was out, so I tried to cross."

"Man, the bridge isn't out. You didn't check your signs.

The road goes up yonder," Upman pointed across the stream. "There's a fork back there to a pontoon bridge just around the bend."

"But isn't this the road?"

"No. It never was. Folks still try to come this way, though we've got it marked—perfectly clear—with a WRONG WAY sign."

"Wasn't there a bridge here yesterday?"

"No sir."

"Then why don't they do something to fix the road instead of just letting it run into the mud like this?"

"It is fixed, I tell you. You just picked the wrong place to cross. Seems like lots of folks bound for the transmitter try to cross here. They're in such a hurry, they barrel right ahead past the signs and get stuck. Of course you hit high water. . . ." He looked at the Mustang. "Your little car'll be needing a bath. Are those your clubs there?"

"No," said Chris. "They belong to another guy. He was with me, but I guess he went back."

"Lots do. Here, let me give you a hand up."

"Thanks," said Chris. "Tell me, what do you call this piece of water?"

Upman grinned, took off his metal hat, and wiped his head with a bandanna. "They call it Stuck Creek," he said. "Now, you get in your car there and I'll tow you to the village—it's not far."

"Wait a minute," said Chris. "How come you're doing all this?"

"You're on your way to that transmitter over there, aren't you?"

"Well—"

"I got my orders to help you get there, that's all."

Chris thought about that. "Who gave you the orders?"

"They're right here." Upman pulled a New Testament from his pocket.

Chris started to feel sick again. What was he getting into? Finally he managed, "Have you been up to this transmitter place?"

"Been there? Man, I've been all the way to Life City!"

Chapter 3

UPMAN brought the Mustang in tow to the small unincorporated settlement of Weathervane, consisting of a gas pump, a garage and a tavern. While the car was gone over inside and out, Chris (his stomach having somewhat recovered) entered the *I Know You*—that being the name of the tavern—and inquired for food. A beef sandwich was shortly placed before him, and while he attacked it a man on the end stool at the bar began chatting with him. This person, rather elderly and possessed of a bulbous nose and white chin whiskers, was the only other customer. He introduced himself as Guy Wise, a retired real estate operator who lived in Carnapolis. He made as if to come closer, but Chris warned him away.

"Better stay where you are," he said. "You might not like the breeze."

"What happened to you?"

"You know where that roadwork is back there by Stuck Creek?"

"Don't tell me you tried to ford it?"

Chris nodded. "My car's across the street getting fixed. Now if I can just find someone to fix me up."

"Son, what made you try it?"

"Various reasons. Mainly, I've got this ache, this funny pressure on my back, and I'm on my way to get some help for it."

"Man, what you need is a drink. Give this friend of mine something," said Wise to the bartender, but Chris waved him away. "Where," the man pursued, "do you reckon to get rid of your trouble? You won't find any back specialists around here. I know some good ones in Carnapolis, though."

"There are specialists in Doomsdale too, but I think I have a better lead," said Chris. "There's a man up at that transmitter who's supposed to know the answers."

Guy Wise put down his glass. "What idiot told you that?" he asked.

"Fellow named van Gelst. I have his card here."

"I thought so." The older man's nostrils twitched as he caught the aroma from Chris' sleeve. "Listen to me! That fellow has stirred up more trouble in these parts than anyone I know. They ought to lock him up. He goes around the county giving crazy advice to strangers and getting them into one jam after another. Look at your gear! You can thank him for that. You keep on listening to him and you're in for a batch."

"Well," said Chris, chewing thoughtfully, "I don't know that I can blame him for what happened back there. It was my own carelessness."

"Son," said Guy Wise, "don't take offense. You don't know me, but I'm older than you are and I've lived around these

parts all my life. This fellow is just no good. Forget about
him. Go on back home. Where you from, Doomsdale? I
thought so. That's a nice town; I own a piece of property
over there. Still travel that way once in a while. Fact is, I
came through there this morning. A real pretty place, with
shade trees and all. But if I told you what lies ahead of you
out this way—if I told you what I know about that transmitter crowd—well, you wouldn't—"

The burden's Pie.
Rogue

"I really don't care, Mr. Wise," said Chris as he pointed to
a piece of pie. "This thing with my back is worse than all
the trouble you can talk about, as far as I'm concerned, and
I'll do anything—I mean *anything*—to get rid of it."

"How long have you had it?"

"Well, to be honest, it started one day last week while I
was trying to do some reading."

"Uh-huh. What were you reading?"

"The New Testament."

"There you go. I thought so. One of those there psychosomatic ailments that start in a man's mind."

"It doesn't hurt any less because of that."

"Don't suppose it does." Guy Wise took a card out of his
wallet and began writing on it. "Tell you what you do,
Anders. You make a left turn fifty yards down the road here,
and go on up the hill a spell till you come to a village called
Upper Striving. Got that? There's a psychologist there who
happens to be my next door neighbor in Carnapolis, but he
keeps office hours in this village. This man, I mean, he knows
just about everything. I figure he can pinpoint your back
business better than any specialist could ever do. He talks
to me a lot about these things. I'm just kind of an amateur,
see, but you sound like a textbook case to me. It may take a

little time, but he'll get you shut of that pain and send you home so good you'll wonder why you ever left. You take this card and forget van what's-his-name. I can tell you right now, I've been over to that transmitter and they don't know anything. They don't know which way is up."

"A headshrinker? What's his name?"

Legal

"Doctor Liegel. He's no phony, Anders. He took his clinical training in Vienna. He's real big-time, but like I say, he prefers to operate in this little town. I sold him the building, and you'll find it right on the main street. What more could you ask for?"

"I'll buy," said Chris. "He sounds good."

"You sure can't go wrong," said Guy Wise, emptying the bottle into his glass. "There's a motel on the edge of town, and a men's wear store near the traffic light. You go up a grade to get there, but you won't have any trouble. What you might do, if your car's ready, is stay there tonight and look him up in the morning. Use that card. If the receptionist knows that Guy Wise sent you, she'll let you go right in."

But as it turned out, Chris never did make it. He finally took delivery of the car in the late afternoon, started out, made the left turn, and headed up the grade. But before he had gone half a mile a sign appeared saying SLIDE AREA. To his consternation he came to a roadbed covered with stones which had washed down the steep cut during the cloudburst of the night before. He picked his way among them for a few hundred yards, until he had to stop the car to move the larger rocks out of his path. As he proceeded the profusion of slide debris became thicker and he noticed, as he got in and out of the car, that gashes were beginning to appear on his tires. To add to his predicament, he suddenly rounded a bend to encounter a brush fire blazing on the lower slope. The smoke blew directly across the road, cutting off his view. Chris decided to turn around and was backing and filling in the narrow space when another car loomed through the smoke behind him and nearly ran into him. The driver, after sounding his horn, quickly stopped and got out, and Chris saw to his embarrassment that the car was a Chevelle and the man coming toward him none other than Ernie van Gelst.

"Anders," he said, "what in the world are you doing up here?"

Chris grimaced as he pulled on the wheel. "I have an appointment to see a doctor in Upper Striving," he said, "and I'm about to break it."

"But I sent you to the transmitter. How did you get on this road in the first place?"

Chris stopped tugging at the wheel and leaned back. "If you must know," he said, "I had some car trouble. While I was waiting to have it fixed at the garage back there, I stopped in at the bar across the street, and some old goat sitting there told me about a Doctor Liegel who was a specialist in psychosomatic back problems like mine. So I figured, what could I lose?"

"My friend," said van Gelst, "you lost just about everything. What was this man's name?"

"Guy Wise. He says he knows you."

"Does he, now? What did he say about me?"

Chris stared straight ahead. "He said you were a kind of religious fanatic who went all over the county giving bad advice to strangers, and that you ought to be put away somewhere. He said he had been up to the transmitter and that they didn't know which way was up."

Van Gelst walked around in front of the Mustang and began pushing away stones with his foot. "Let's get these cars turned around," he said, "and then I'd like to spend some time with you."

They maneuvered their cars back away from the fire and came slowly down the hill until visibility cleared and the rocks were less menacing. Here they pulled into a turnout, and van Gelst came over and sat beside Chris.

"Anders," he asked, "why did you leave Doomsdale?"

"Well," said Chris, "I thought I had a purpose when I left, but right now I could probably be psyched into admitting I took a runout."

"But you had this physical problem, you said."

"Still have it."

"What else troubled you?"

"The state of the world. I figure now it's only a matter of hours before the big bombs start dropping that'll put an end to us."

"But other people were disturbed, and they didn't leave."

Chris fidgeted with the steering wheel. "I guess I meant to look for something. Or someone."

"God?"

"Well, yes, in a way."

How can you explain to someone you don't know that you're sick and tired of yourself and have been for forty-three years How do you say I came to the end of the line and didn't care about anyone or anything Just wanted to cop out and go look for whoever started it all and try to find out what went wrong I give up I can't explain anything. . . .

"Are you still looking for him?" Chris did not answer. "Do you believe God can help you?" persisted van Gelst.

Chris stuck out his lower lip. "I believe only the Lord can straighten out this fouled-up world situation."

"And will he?"

"Why—"

"I'm going to put it to you straight, Anders," said van Gelst. "Your problem is not the world, it's you, and you know it. But you've just about hamstrung yourself. The advice you followed was all bad. And yet this fellow Guy Wise is not an unpleasant person. I know him. I believe he attends a church over in Struggletown, which isn't far from Carnapolis. But he did three things that came close to finishing you off."

"What three things?" asked Chris, suddenly feeling very tired.

"First of all, he got you off the right road. When a man is on the kind of journey you're on, it's sudden death to sidetrack him. The search requires everything he has; it calls up every cell in his body. If he turns off to one side or the other, it's fatal. Second, he sent you on the wrong road. He directed you to Doctor Liegel and told you he could handle your case. Liegel is a quack. He wasn't trained in Vienna. He isn't a clinical psychologist. He has a few analytic techniques that he learned from a book and applies woodenly to everyone who comes to him. He says, 'Follow my rules and you'll be cured.' He hardly looks at his patients. Never in a thousand years will he get that trouble out of your back, because what you've got, according to the book in my hand, is not something even good psychology or psychiatry can treat. You have a spiritual sickness.

"Now Liegel will tell you differently. He'll try to make it sound as if you have a psychosomatic condition, and he'll say,

'Your pain is caused by a guilt feeling. You need to give yourself an out.' He's right that your pain is related to a sense of guilt, but he's wrong in thinking you can shrug it off. That only makes it worse. Liegel likes to tell his people, 'Get rid of your inhibitions and you'll feel better.' That's not true. It's the worst legalism of all, because it has no morals."

"I know it's a lie," said Chris, "because I've tried it. If that's all that doctor has to offer, I nearly killed myself for nothing."

"What you ran into on the road to Upper Striving," said van Gelst, "was what every man runs into when he sets out to solve his problems by himself. They used to call it bootstrap religion, and it has never worked and never will. The only way to God is the way God himself has made. And that's the third mistake your friend Guy Wise made."

"What was that?"

"He ignored the directions."

"What direction?"

"God's directions."

"But we never even talked about God."

"Exactly."

"He said he could help me get fixed up so I could go back to my family in Doomsdale."

"And he lied. Let me read you something: 'No man, having put his hand to the plow, and looking back, is fit for the kingdom of God.' You see, you're not just on another experimental project, Anders. The computers will never get this program. This one is for keeps."

"Yeah? Well, maybe I'm not ready for keeps. I'm married, you know. I've got a wife and four boys back there."

"They haven't been forgotten."

"You bet they haven't. I know everybody thinks I ditched my family, but that wasn't the idea at all. What I told Eileen was, I wanted to get away and get some help. It sounds crazy, now I think of it, but at the time I had been reading the Bible, and then there was all the war business. I guess it made me panic. You just try living with this thing on your back and see how you react!"

"Look, if you will just turn left up here at the intersection—"

"I'm sick of the driving conditions around here. No matter which way I turn, I'm in trouble. I think maybe I just ought to go back and see how they're getting along, and then try to get some help in Doomsdale. It was probably a mistake to leave. There must be somebody there who can feed me a pill that will give me some relief."

"You forget, you tried there."

"Well, at least I can get cleaned up. I can't stand the smell of myself." He turned the key and started up his engine, but van Gelst reached over and quietly shut it off.

"I know why you want to go back," he said. "You're not kidding anyone."

"What do you mean, you know? I don't know myself."

"You've got some problems there that won't leave you alone. But I can tell you that you're in no shape to handle them, Anders. You'll just stir up the mud."

"Yeah? You seem to know a lot."

Van Gelst grinned. "Your friend Guy Wise was right, you need to get yourself fixed up. But don't listen to him—don't listen to anybody. Just keep going the way you started."

"When do I head back to Doomsdale, then?"

"Forget all about Doomsdale." Van Gelst's expression changed. "Forget about everything except this. Man, you're blind; and the Bible says when one blind man tries to lead another, they both end up in the ditch."

"You mean forget about my wife and the boys? What kind of monster are you?"

"Naturally I didn't mean forget them. Look, would you like to get rid of that back pressure for good and all? Would you like something that will make a new man of you? I'm talking about today."

Chris looked sideways at him. "You gave me that sweet talk before," he said.

"But you got off the road. You have to follow the directions and watch where you're going. That's basic."

"OK, let's have it once more. Slower this time."

"Right. You go back to Weathervane, get on the main county road and follow it across the valley and up the hill. When you come to the summit there's a radio transmitter. The call letters are WEAL. Right below the tower you'll see the transmitter station. There's an engineer on duty there, his name is Colonel Goodall. You tell him who you are and why you've come. Got it?"

"I think so. Has he got a shower?"

"Yes." He offered his hand. "God in your heart."

Van Gelst went back to his Chevelle, and Chris once again put his Mustang on the road, muttering to himself, "So help me, if anybody else tries to take me up the garden path. . . . "

And they did try. When he stopped at Weathervane, there was Guy Wise standing in front of the *I Know You*, watching for him and hollering as he swung to the left and moved down the county road. A mile further along a car was stranded on the opposite shoulder, its hood up, and a man stood there waving. This time Chris slowed down.

"I just need a little push," the man said. "I'm trying to get to Doomsdale."

"Get in," said Chris. "I'll run you back to the garage."

"How far is it?"

"A mile or so."

"No, no, I mean, how far is it to Doomsdale?"

"Oh, maybe twenty-five miles. That's my town—or it was."

The man's face came alive. "Say," he said, "would you tow me there? I'll pay you whatever you ask. Fifty bucks? Look, I've got a good towrope in the trunk."

"You don't want the garage?" asked Chris.

"No, I'm late to an appointment. But I really will—"

Chris moved the stick in to D. "Sorry," he said. "I'm a little late myself." He sped across the valley and began climbing the hill where the tower was now clearly visible, its warning light flashing. Dusk seemed to be settling fast; a mist came up from the lowlands and obscured the summit as he reached it. However, his directions were accurate; the car turned in through a grove of trees and headed up to a low building below the transmitter, marked only by the letters above the door, WEAL.

As Chris began to slow down there was a sudden violent clap of thunder and immediately a tattoo began beating on the roof of the car. Hail almost the size of mothballs was now falling and clattering around him. He pulled on the brake, leaped out into the pelting storm and made a dash for the doorway.

Chapter 4

AS CHRIS reached the entrance to the transmitter building a light flashed on over the doorway. The door opened, an arm reached out, seized him, and pulled him in; whereupon the door slammed shut. Chris shakily recovered his balance and found himself in a passageway formed of concrete blocks, facing a husky, unsmiling young man who wore fatigues and jangled a set of keys on an enormous ring.

"What was that all about?" demanded Chris, brushing the drops from his eyes and hair.

"Thank God you're here, sir," was the reply in a rather strange accent. "This operation is under constant attack by the Principalities, and one of their weapons is short-range weather control. When they turn it on it takes us a few moments to neutralize it. Last night we lost two people right at our doorstep."

"Who's doing all this? Where's the sheriff? What's the matter with the National Guard?"

"Sir," said the young man, swinging his key ring toward the other end of the hall, "I have orders to conduct you to a guest apartment. A shower, some food and a night's lodging will be provided. If you will let me have your keys, your luggage will be brought to you in a few minutes, as soon as the hail has stopped. Colonel Goodall will see you in the morning. This way, please."

Chris followed his guide through the concrete building and noticed that it had the bleak appearance of a military underground defense establishment. An elevator took them down two levels, where the atmosphere brightened considerably. Contemporary prints began to appear on attractive walls; the floors were covered; soft lighting came from recessed lamps. He was shown into a tastefully appointed room in two tones of gray with a comfortable-looking bed, drapes, tapestries and a plush carpet. On the far wall hung a modest print of Christ and his disciples. A television set stood in the corner.

"We have ordered a prime rib dinner for you, with salad, coffee and dessert," said the young man. "I see your clothes are in rather bad shape. If you will leave them outside the door they'll be ready for you in the morning."

"You must have quite a staff," murmured Chris. "What is this place, a fort or something? Are you in the service?"

"Yes sir, on six months volunteer duty. This whole emplacement is manned by volunteers. We are here to see that everyone who comes through gets the same kind of treatment. You'll find a Bible on the dresser. Have a good rest." And he was gone.

Within less than an hour the offending garments were in the hallway and Chris, having soaked under the hot shower and partaken of an excellent meal which appeared at the door on a tray, was easing his grateful body between the cool sheets.

At six-thirty the next morning the television set suddenly came to life with a flashing of WEAL station signals and a fanfare of bugle calls. Chris squinted at the set and discovered a man eyeballing him from the screen. "Good morning, Mr. Anders," said the face. "I hope you enjoyed your rest. Your laundry is just outside the door. Orange juice will be brought to you in forty-five minutes, and at eight o'clock you will be given an escort to the commandant's office. I am the commandant." The set went blank.

Chris swung his legs over the bed and winced. His hand went instinctively to his back. Yesterday's immersion had been an experience he would pay for. As he stood again under the shower he began to wonder why he had ever thought that leaving home might be a solution to his problems. As if you could run away from the menace of Red China! He found himself thinking about the last camping trip he had taken with the boys, before the older ones had drifted from him. He thought of the way Eileen would fix a Sunday morning breakfast with waffles and honey.

Promptly at eight he was escorted by another young volunteer to the elevator and taken down a level to a steel slab that peeled back in a synchronized movement with the elevator door, disclosing a private office. "Come in," said a hearty voice, and Chris found himself confronted by a pleasant-looking individual of about fifty who introduced himself as Colonel Goodall. Chris recognized the face as the one that (had roused him from his bed via the TV set. The Colonel wore a well-tailored gray suit. His office, apart from a certain

Spartan quality, might have been any executive suite. An engineering diploma hung on one wall, and an astrolabe was mounted in a corner. On the corner of the desk was a Bible. The only other unusual feature was a population clock which ticked away behind the desk, apparently recording the balance of deaths and births. Chris was invited to seat himself in a comfortable chair.

"Where are you from, Mr. Anders?" inquired the Colonel.

"Doomsdale, actually," said Chris. "This whole business seems to have started at home one night last week while I was reading the New Testament."

"That's a normal pattern," nodded Goodall. "What were you reading?"

"A passage near the end of Revelation, I think. I've been meaning to look it up. I don't know the Bible too well, though I took a course in it. But it was something about a judgment that was coming and a place called Life City, as I remember. Then while I was sitting there, a kind of burning started up between my shoulder blades. This thing has bothered me off and on in the past, but that night I tell you it sent me right up the wall."

"Did you take a sedative? Aspirin?"

"Drugs never helped me much before, and I couldn't see why they would now. It was just one more thing added to a lot of others. So I just decided to start out. I didn't know where, or why, but—"

"What did you do with your family?"

"I left them in Doomsdale. I offered to bring them along, but they weren't interested. The fact is, my wife and I—"

"Who directed you here?" interrupted Goodall again.

"Fellow named van Gelst," said Chris. "But when I tried

to follow his directions I ran my Mustang into a stinking creek. If it hadn't been for a road crew man who happened along, I'd be there yet."

"Ah, yes, that would be Upman. A splendid fellow. Did anyone come with you?"

"I started out with a neighbor named Warren Clay, who said he was interested in where I was going. Then when we got stuck in midstream he waded off and left me."

"Was your car damaged?"

"Oh, once we got out we had to haul it to Weathervane and have it worked on. It was a mess."

"And then you drove up here?"

"Well, not exactly. I met this old gaffer who told me about somebody who lives in Upper Striving—a Doctor Liegel, I think—who's supposed to know a lot about cases like mine."

"You mean you left the road?"

"Well, in a way, yes. I thought he was giving me a good steer, but I ran into such conditions on the road—you wouldn't believe it if I told you. Rocks—a landslide, and then a brush fire—I thought for a while I was done for. But finally I got turned around. Never did get to see that man."

"You got some bad advice. Everyone knowns Liegel is a phony. So is the man who talked to you, Guy Wise. It seems to me you wandered around quite a bit, Anders. What else happened?"

"Oh, while I was backing and turning, van Gelst showed up from somewhere and steered me back on the highway. I didn't have any trouble after that until I got right up here to the top of the hill. I ran into a lot of mist, and then while I was parking the car the sky fell in."

"I'm glad you made it," said the Colonel. At this point

a paneled door opened and a girl attendant, from some Asian country, Chris thought, rolled in a cart with coffee and Danish pastry. She smiled at him, and he noted that she too was wearing fatigues. As she poured him a cup of coffee and the aroma came to his nostrils, he felt himself relaxing for the first time in what seemed an age. A flicker of hope went through him.

"Do you think, Colonel," he began, "that I might get some help for this—"

"Cream?" asked the smiling attendant.

"Oh, yes. And sugar."

"Yes," said Goodall genially, "you'll get help. If you get where you're going, the pain will go away of itself."

"Where's that?"

"You'll be told."

"Colonel, just what kind of club are you running here?"

"We can't describe the nature of our operation, Mr. Anders, except to say it is concerned with Outer Space and is not related to Cape Kennedy. We're set up to service people like yourself who are on the road to Life City. We take in anyone. A number of individuals have arrived even since you came last night."

"But it seems to be a war—all these people shuttling about in uniform—does the Pentagon know about this?"

"Some men in the Pentagon know about it. It is a war, certainly, as you will find out."

"Don't tell me I'm going to be inducted at my age. Flabby old me?"

"No, we'll keep you here just long enough to put you through a briefing session. That will be with Major Putter in our staff room on the next level. After that you're on your way. First, however, I want to say one or two things about your passport that may be helpful to you."

"About my what?"

"Excuse me, Mr. Anders. About the Bible." And the Colonel began to speak matter-of-factly, without any pulpit mannerisms or holy tones, about the meaning of certain passages of Scripture. Chris listened carefully. It seemed to him that in all the hours he had spent listening to religiously minded people, the real teaching of the Word of God had never been expounded to him so simply and clearly. He managed to put in a question or two, particularly about the person of the Holy Spirit. He found himself wondering why it had taken so many years for him to find a man with whom he could sit and have an unembarrassed talk about things always, in his experience, considered either too sacred or too silly to be mentioned.

Finally the Colonel closed his Bible and pressed a buzzer. The escort Chris had met on his arrival reappeared. "This is Philip," Goodall explained. "He will take you to the studio." He held out his hand. "God in your heart," he said.

The sign on the door opposite the elevator shaft read simply N. T. R. PUTTER. Philip opened it and escorted Chris into a well-lighted staff room filled with blackboards, maps, charts, tables, clocks, globes, anemometers and scale models of the celestial regions. A large white screen was built into one wall, and slide and film projects dominated the center of the room along with three studio chairs.

A dapper, balding man in uniform emerged briskly from an adjoining room and nodded to Chris. He spoke with a BBC accent, and his upper lip supported a hairline mustache. "How do you do," he said. "I'm Major Putter. If you will be seated, Philip will turn out the lights and we shall proceed with the briefing." The Major's clipped, even tones as he continued cut through the darkness like a saw.

"Firstly, old chap, we shall make use of the slide projector. This first scene is rather nice, I'd say." It turned out to be a colored slide of a sunny mountain meadow, with a family seated on a rock in the foreground. The scene was one of breathtaking beauty. "This photograph," said the Major, "tries to express in a symbolic way what God has in store for you. It tells you that your Creator wishes to make of your life a thing of radiance."

The next slide brought a grunt from Chris. It showed him the yellow Mustang mired in the creek with dirty water swirling around it. "You might recognize this scene," said the Major with a gentle cough. "This is man as he tries to run his own life. The polluted stream, of course, is human sin. I believe this makes rather a useful illustration and I plan to use it again."

"My pleasure," muttered Chris.

The frame changed, and a reproduction of Gordon's "Calvary" came in view. "We are not certain that this is the exact archaeological site outside Jerusalem where the crucifixion took place," said the Major, "but it does very well for our purposes. The Bible teaches that here around the year 30 A.D. a change took place in the moral nature of the universe."

"What was that?" asked Chris.

"Jesus Christ died on the cross for our sins," said the Major simply. "We have two more slides, and then a film."

The fourth photograph was another shocker for Chris. It was taken at his high-school graduation years before. He was standing on the stage of the Doomsdale High Auditorium, holding out his hand for the diploma that was being presented to him. "This picture symbolizes the meaning of salvation," said the Major. "It shows you in the act of accepting. God gives; we receive. Now for one final picture. Notice the features of this person when he appears." The person who flashed into view could have been any businessman on the morning shuttle between New York and Washington; but Chris gave an exclamation.

"I know that fellow," he said. "I just can't place him."

"This man," said Major Putter, "is a qualified and authorized guide. You will meet him along the way. He ranks at the top of our personnel list."

"Who is he?" asked Chris.

Major Putter flicked the switch. "All in due time, my dear man. Any other questions?"

"Why, uh, yes—" Chris began.

"It doesn't matter," said the Major, breaking in neatly. "The film you are about to see will explain most of the points that are giving you difficulty. It will show, for example, why you were wasting your time trying to get to Upper Striving. It will demonstrate how Liegel's so-called 'cures' only make the patient worse. It will spell out the difference between passion and patience. And it will explain the properties and uses of spiritual oil."

"Spiritual oil—what's that? Some kind of lube job? Are you going to give me a tune-up, Major?"

The Major chose to ignore him. "The scenes that follow will be a bit violent, I'm afraid. You will learn something of the military strategy of the Principalities. After that there will be some related themes, and a final sequence in a dungeon of the Château d'If."

The projector turned on with a roar, and the Major stepped back into his office leaving Chris exposed to a battery of sights and sounds certainly unique in his experience. He wondered if what he was watching was what the French called "total cinema." Scenes jumped back and forth and blended into each other until at times it was impossible to tell what subject was being treated; yet the effect was unmistakable and convincing.

In the early reels the whole history of man's religious efforts was evoked in kaleidoscopic form. Sequence after sequence portrayed the titanic struggle of individuals in human history to reach the portals of Heaven by means of prayers, gods, shrines, idols, gates, towers, monuments, fasts, regulations, pilgrimages and sacred paraphernalia. One by one each effort tottered and collapsed, leaving mankind worse off than before. Then the film rehearsed in symbols the sin of man's first parents and showed the demonic sources of human pride, and how it inevitably fostered one war after another.

As the picture continued to unwind, Chris saw a few clips he thought he recognized from *The Robe, The Gospel According to Matthew* and *The Greatest Story Ever Told*. In these scenes and others, the film intimated with exquisite restraint what it could not represent: the spiritual meaning of Christmas, Good Friday and Easter. A master of cinema art seemed to have realized that he could not screen the unscreenable except by suggestion and a touch of love. Then came the Council of Jerusalem—a snatch of it—and the scene shifted quickly to the Circus Maximus in Rome, with the crowds crying for the blood of Christians and wild beasts padding up and down subterranean passages waiting to be let out. In the midst of the arena he saw a squalid band of Christians, utterly desolate, and heard a voice whisper to them, "God in your heart."

Suddenly he was back in the twentieth century, and two men in what looked like Nazi uniforms were standing in front of a burning brick wall, trying to put out the blaze with a fire hose. The stream played on the flames, but the more water they poured on the wall, the higher the flames leaped. Then the camera panned around to the other side of the wall, revealing a series of oil ducts penetrating through the bricks and connected with a drum of crude oil, which obviously kept the fire burning. Four men in coveralls were continually rolling up fresh drums and replacing the supply. Chris noticed that the drums had been stenciled GRACE OIL CO., and as the camera moved in closer he could see names stitched on the men's coverall pockets: *Luke, Matthew, John* and *Mark.*

At last the parade of symbols drew to an end and the scene shifted to the Château d'If, where a bearded man was sitting in a cold, damp dungeon, half-clothed in rags that had obviously not been changed in years. His fingernails were uncut, his eyes nearly caked shut with dirt, his skin covered with sores, his feet swollen and crippled, and he seemed either unable or unwilling to move. Behind him was an open door and a large sign which read EXIT. A shaft of sunlight could be seen coming through the passage. Yet there he sat; and after a few moments he began to speak through darkened, rotting teeth.

"Oh yes," he said, "I believed. I thought I was going to Life City. But here I am. I know now I'll never make it."

He sighed, and there followed another painful silence.

"I know that door. But I tell you I can't walk through it.

The Bible says to repent, but I can't. I had my chance. Now it's gone. As least I feel it's gone. And when I think about what lies ahead. . . . "

The film went into a series of flashes; it was finished. The Major, who had slipped into the room, now switched off the projector and turned up the lights. "That's it," he said. "You're free to go."

Chris sat in his chair, stunned. "What kind of ending is that?" he demanded. "How can you leave a man sitting there without hope? What are you trying to tell me?"

"The Christian life is not a game, my dear Mr. Anders. The stakes are high." He pointed to a large, black octagonal can of film on a rack behind him. "There is another film here I can show you if you insist upon it. It's a representation of what the Bible says are things to come—in full color. But you won't like it."

Chris shuddered. "I've seen enough," he said. "Which way is out?"

"Oh yes, of course. Do you recall by any chance what time it was when you picked up that New Testament back in Doomsdale?" asked the Major.

"No, I don't."

The Major glanced at a chart on the wall. "Let's see—according to your profile it was eight forty-three in the evening," he said. He stepped over to a large astronomically timed wall clock, and moved the hands ahead to 8:43. Then he stepped to a computer control and typed a series of numbers. A plastic-covered card emerged from the machine and was handed to Chris. "Keep this," the Major said. Whereupon he pressed another button, and an opening perhaps four feet square appeared in the floor in front of the screen, with steps leading down. The Major picked up two flashlights and handed one to Chris and the other to Philip, who was waiting quietly.

"We are developing an electronic device that neutralizes the missile firepower of the Principalities by jamming," the Major explained. "It's still in the experimental stage, but it's built on what we call the apostolic principle—Paul spells it out in 1 Corinthians 10:13. We haven't quite solved the time lag yet. Now Philip will conduct you to the exit," he added and offered his hand. "God in your heart," he said.

"Major Putter," said Chris, "you have been kind."

"Not at all."

Following his guide, Chris descended the wooden steps and was then led through a half-mile of lighted concrete passageway which seemed to twist in aimless fashion. At last they came to an impressive steel gate that blocked the end of the tunnel. In it was a small notch, into which Philip inserted one of the keys on his large ring. Before turning it he faced about and regarded Chris.

"This will let you out on the side of the hill," he said. "Our summit is connected to a higher one by a ridge, and that's your only way. There's a slight drop before you start to climb. Aim for the top. The trail is easy to follow, but you'd better get a running start. We never know what will happen."

"What about my clothes? What about the Mustang?" asked Chris in some alarm.

Philip shook his head. "Driving is too dangerous for you," he said. "You've got to get off this hill in one piece. Remember what the Major said about the time lag. We have detectors that can give our staff people advance warning when they're outside, but they would not help you. We'll get your things together and have them waiting, locked in your car in a parking area at the bottom of the next hill. Here are your keys—we have our own set—and here's a map of the ridge trail. All you have to remember is, stay on the trail and move fast."

"If you say so," said Chris.

"One other thing."

"What's that?"

"You won't go alone."

"Are you coming?"

"No. But you will have an invisible means of support."

"Thanks."

Philip opened the small steel door and let Chris out. "God in your heart," he said. "Run!"

Chapter 5

AS HE dashed out of the tunnel Chris found himself on a dirt path leading down through a grove of oak trees. A greenish mist obscured the slope, punctuated by occasional bright flashes. There was an odd smell in the air. Glancing up, he noticed something bright streaking through the sky about two hundred feet over his head. It was followed by another streak and another, each coming closer to him. They looked like tracer bullets. It occurred to Chris that the Principalities might be taking their sport by firing UFO's at him; and the thought of a supernatural war being waged against his body filled him with terror. Another flash went by, this time so close that he ducked instinctively. Then came a stabbing pain full in the back and he knew he had been hit. The ground vibrated beneath his feet. He lurched off the trail and staggered into a tree.

Oh oh oh oh they got me where it hurts I'm cooked How did they know What happened What hit me My back's broken in

*two How can I get out of here The devil's caught up with me
Always knew he would I'll never give him the slip Never be
any good Might better have stayed in Doomsdale.* . . .

In disengaging himself from the tree-trunk he tripped on
a root and fell sprawling. As he lay there an unhealthy warm
odor rose from the ground, making him gag and choke. With
a superhuman effort he pulled himself up by the young oak
tree and started back to the trail. The shooting pains were
beginning to affect his optic nerves, but he could see well
enough to continue downhill. "I'll make it, I'll make it," he
muttered between coughs, "or go down swinging."

At that moment a raucous flock of starlings appeared from
nowhere and began dive-bombing him, pecking at his head
and tearing his clothes. When he fought them off, the birds
screeched louder than ever and went for his eyes. He was
forced to cover his face with his hands and run blindly, rico-
cheting off one tree, then another. "No!" he cried. "They'll
never get me. I won't let 'em. No. No!" And again he
stumbled and fell, and again the noxious odor of the earth
began to choke him and forced him, staggering, to his feet.
Then he remembered: the guard said if they had time, they
could neutralize the attacks.

He became half-hysterical; swinging his elbows back and
forth against the flapping birds as he ran, he bawled out,
"God! Neutralize! Neutralize!" The hill suddenly leveled
off under his feet and he was in the clear. The attackers disappeared as quickly as they had come. Chris opened his
fingers and peered through them. His vision was returning.
He found he had reached the saddle of the ridge and was only
a few yards from the trail, which stretched out and up before
him, heading toward another summit perhaps a thousand

feet above. The green mist clung to the hill behind him. The sky looked down benignly. He bent over with difficulty, picked up a clod of earth and smelled it; it was cool and sweet.

Chris found a rock, sat down with a wince and a grunt, and examined himself tenderly. The ray or whatever it was that struck his back had caused an additional angry swelling along his upper spine. He felt almost humpbacked. The birds had drawn blood in about twenty places; his hair was caked and matted; his clothes had been plucked until they were rags. Yet in spite of his pains he felt a strange sense of exhilaration, as if he had been delivered from all the demons of hell. He swabbed at his wounds as best he could, then gingerly rose to his feet and started up the trail.

It took Chris several hours to make his way up the mountain. He was forced into a stoop by the swelling on his neck and back; moreover, his feet bothered him, and he was astonished to discover that the soles had been burned off both shoes. When the trail became stony, it was not long before he was leaving telltale red marks on the path; but he hardly noticed the added pain, so intent was he on reaching the summit. As he approached the peak something about the topography began to take on an air of familiarity. It remained a mystery until he rounded a bend and came to the base of a forty-foot cliff, which he recognized as the one he had seen in the photograph on Major Putter's slide projector. It was Gordon's Calvary.

The most prominent feature of the cliff was the skull face, where indentations marked the eye sockets and cheek bones. Above it was a level place that might have been used by the Romans for execution purposes. "Not exactly established as the authentic site," the Major had said, "but it does very well for our purposes." Chris stared at the cliff, then began the final ascent around it to the top. He knew of course that there would be no crosses on the summit, no holes where crosses had been, nothing whatever in fact except a bare and windswept place. Yet a deep-borne instinct made him drag his way, bent as he was, up the final incline until he stood on the highest ground.

Like any good climber, he spent a moment gazing at the view from the top—north, west, south and east. So this was Calvary! The place where, according to Major Putter, a moral change had been brought about in the universe. The Place of the Skull. The Jerusalem city dump. The bald peak where curs and foxes once gathered at night to leap at the entrails of dangling corpses. The scene of the Good Friday earthquake. The despised place, the place of loathsomeness, where hapless criminals shed cheap blood and Rome kept its mailed hand on Israel's throat. He had read about it in Bible lit, long ago.

As he looked around the small area of the summit, Chris wondered why God would choose such a forsaken spot to bring Heaven and earth together. He wondered whether he could ever leap the moral and intellectual picket fence that had kept him out of Christianity in the past. For the hundreth time he asked himself how it was possible for sins to be forgiven through the death of one man—*here*. Did God really "lay upon his Son the iniquity of us all"? Did Christ really make a "full, perfect and sufficient sacrifice for the offenses of the whole world, the innocent for the guilty, the just for the unjust, to bring us to God"—as he had heard in church so often in his boyhood?

What did happen back there That's what I want to know Jesus said "It is finished" but what was finished How can a man who has been wrong all his life suddenly be made right zap like that Who says he's right God but if God pardons a man does that mean the man is now right or is it just that God is soft-hearted I remember something in that movie What was it A book I think they called it the Ledger of Life and I remember somebody's hand kept transferring entries from God's account on one page to Abraham's account on the next page and I thought Now that looks like pretty fancy bookkeeping but the voice kept saying "Abraham believed God and it was reckoned to him as righteousness" and then there was something about when we're justified by God it's more than a pardon The penalty of sin was not simply waived How did it go At the cross the demands of the law of God were fully satisfied by God himself but if Jesus Christ did die to take away sin why didn't he take away the sins of all these dictators so they wouldn't be threatening to spray poison on the planet That's what I want to know. . . .

Problems everywhere, and apparently no solutions available on this hill or anywhere else. Chris looked over toward the lower eminence where the transmitter stood. The green mist still blanketed its base, and he could see occasional streaks darting through it. "Somebody else getting the business," he thought, fingering the sores on his arms. Then he noticed that the red light on the transmitter was flashing an odd pattern. As he studied it, he saw it blinking three quick flashes and then a long, sustained flash. Three shorts, one long. The light on a transmitter tower, he knew, was nothing more than an aircraft warning beacon. It had no business signaling. But just suppose the people in that place were trying to get a message to him without running the gantlet of UFO artillery. What kind a message would it be? Something spiritual. . . .

Spiritual! Now he was clicking. What was it Colonel Goodall had said about the Holy Spirit? The problems in the Bible —all these questions about a man getting right with God— were spiritual matters and the answers did not come by logic or reason but from the Spirit of God himself. He, Chris, had not started away from Doomsdale just to "bug out"; he had started first of all because the Spirit of God was drawing him. That's what the Colonel had said. The whole thing was already worked out in the counsels of God. So here he was at Gordon's Calvary, and here was this light trying to tell him something: three shorts, one long.

Victory! Of course. The victory sign. But whose victory? Spiritual victory? A quiver went through him, and he suddenly realized that his body was no longer bending forward, that watching the light he had unconsciously straightened up, and that for at least five minutes he had felt no pain in his back.

"Why, what—" he began. Then he shouted. "God! You've done it! You've done it!" But he couldn't believe it. His thumbs reached around to touch his shoulder blades; everything was back to normal. He punched upward at his spine with his fist; there was no soreness. "Man!" he hollered, and began to dance about in his bird-spattered rags; but his feet hurt and the torn clothes tripped him. In a moment or two his knees buckled; he bowed his head, and the tears began to flow. Whatever was wrong with the world, whatever Calvary was about, he knew that in the twinkling of an eye he, Chris Anders, had become a new creation.

Praise God Thank You Heavenly Father How come me How
come You did it for me I didn't deserve it Lord I'm the most
weak-livered parasite that ever walked into a church I don't
deserve this kind of royal treatment Why would You pass up
all the big people to heal a second-rate computer hustler Oh
Jesus I know I'm a rotten sinner God when I think of what
I've done to You and Eileen and the boys and well even the
dog next door but You didn't care Didn't matter to You what
I did or was You died right here for me I see now what You
did You took my wickedness and laziness and pain and sick-
ness and let them die with You on the cross so I could live
with Your peace and Your love I don't get it Why did You
do it You knew I wasn't worth it I'll never get over it I'm so
happy I could die. . . .

After a long while he straightened his back and, still kneel-
ing, opened his eyes and then his arms. He felt as if he had
fallen in love with the whole world. He wanted to talk, to
sing, to shout, and to do it all at once. But the best he could
come up with was a silly little chorus Dana had brought
home from Sunday School:

> Turn it over to Jesus
> And smile the rest of the day.

At last he got painfully to his feet and tried a few calis-
thenics to test the rest of his body. It remained for the time
mutilated by the jabs of his attackers, but the great burning
pain of his back was gone, and he knew that the burden of
his life had rolled away, instantaneously, completely, perm-
anently. Again he tipped back his head and laughed for sheer
joy. Even his feet seemed better. Again he swiveled his body
from his hips and tried another chorus of Dana's that rushed
into his mind:

Nothing is impossible when you put your trust in God;
Nothing is impossible when you're trusting in his Word.
    Hearken to the voice of God to thee:
    "Is there anything too hard for me?"

Some hikers appeared in view on the trail approaching the summit. There were three of them. Each was stripped to the waist and each wore heavy boots and hiking shorts of forest green. Their bodies shone with a grease of some sort, and they carried full packs. Chris walked toward them, fully conscious that he was a comical sight but refusing to let it disturb his state of ecstasy.

"Praise the Lord," he shouted as the men reached the top. They nodded amicably.

"Praise the Lord," they returned.

"Did you fellows come through that mist down there?"

"No problem," said one. "This grease we have acts as a shield."

"But what about breathing? I almost choked, it was so bad."

The hiker tapped his pack. "Oxygen," he said.

A second hiker held out his hand. "May I extend my congratulations and stamp your forehead?" he asked, smiling. Chris looked at him more closely. There were no marks on the man's face. He grasped the hand, puzzled.

"Thanks, but what's the forehead bit?"

"Just an identification. Nothing to it, but it will help you where you're going."

"Am I going somewhere?" asked Chris.

"I thought you were going to Life City."

"That's right."

"Your car's waiting for you at the foot of the mountain." By this time the man had removed his pack, taken out a rubber stamp, and pressed it on Chris' forehead.

"That'll fix you up," he said.

"What does it say?" asked Chris.

"Sealed," he said, "but you can't read it."

"Sealed?"

"Yup."

The first man to address him had unloaded his pack and now came toward Chris with a load of clothing on his arm.

new clothes "Here you are," the hiker said. "Peel off those duds and get into these."

Chris wasted no time. It took approximately seven seconds to divest himself of the remnants of his wardrobe. Eagerly he slipped into the clean linen and the comfortable green wool outfit. Everything fit perfectly, including soft wool socks and a new pair of hiking boots.

"Marvelous. Absolutely marvelous," he said. "Like wallpaper. How did you know my size?"

"We didn't, but your size is known in Life City. That's where the clothes come from."

The hiker took Chris' rags and stuffed them into his knapsack. "You won't be needing these," he said.

The second hiker, having put away his stamp, now approached Chris with some food and a canteen of water. The food was hardtack and cheese which Chris gratefully accepted. The cakes of hardtack were then passed out to the others and the canteen started following around. Chris, who was acutely conscious of emptiness, had already begun nibbling the cheese when he noticed the other men bowing their heads.

L. supper "We remember Your death," said the second hiker, "until You come."

The simple meal lasted approximately four minutes. No one bothered to be seated. Then as the others were closing the flaps and reshouldering their packs, the third hiker walked over to Chris with a book.

"This is the Bible you were reading back in Doomsdale," he said. "You're to carry it on your journey and then show it at the city gate."

Chris took it and examined it wonderingly. "How'd you ever get hold of that?" he asked.

The hiker smiled. "You'll find out some day. Meanwhile don't lose it. It's your passport!"

Chris thanked him and immediately sat down and began to look up the passage in Revelation that had started up the burning pain in his back. He wanted to be sure it wouldn't happen again. When he found it he read it aloud, half-fearing the worst. Nothing happened. He patted the book, jumped up and began doing another jig despite his painful feet. "I made it," he shouted. When had he ever felt like this? Could he really be forty-three years old? He looked around him. While he was reading, the hikers had quietly returned down the trail.

Chris studied the grass. It seemed greener to him than usual. He wondered whether it really did have all that chlorophyll or whether his eyes were affected, and then remembered another tune little Dana had brought home from Sunday School:

> His name is Wonderful, his name is Wonderful,
> His name is Wonderful, Jesus my Lord.

Singing and whistling, Chris started down the hill. In his trousers pocket he felt the keys to the Mustang. Following the trail map, he took a path that led directly to the bottom. As he descended through a wood, again he had the sensation of being alive to nature in a fresh way. He spotted a cardinal, then a cedar waxwing, then a couple of bluebirds. A chipmunk chattered at him. Lizards seemed to smile at him as they dodged about.

> Bow down before him, love and adore him,
> His name is Wonderful, Jesus my Lord.

Emerging from the wood, he came to a broken-down fence with a sign that read LAZY 3 RANCH. By now he had nearly reached the valley floor and was looking about for the parking area with the Mustang. The trail became a bridle path. It dipped into a slight hollow and Chris found himself in front of a decrepit unpainted building whose false front annouced that it was the LAST CHANCE SALOON. It looked like a prop from a Hollywood ghost town. Chris stuck his head inside the door and discovered three men, bearded and dirty, seated at a table and engaged in a card game. One of them turned half around and stared at him.

"That you doin' all that singin'?" he demanded.

"Yes. I—"

"Beat it," he said, turning back and reshuffling the deck in his hands. Chris glanced around the gloomy interior. Cobwebs were everywhere. The dust lay a quarter-inch thick on the bar. Beetles crawled through cracks in the plank floor.

"Beat it, I said."

Chris looked at the man again and noticed that his ankle was chained to a huge iron ring set in the floor. Similar chains were attached to bands on the other players' legs. It was an incredible sight. Still intoxicated with the new wine of freedom, Chris found it impossible to accept the strange condition of these human beings, trapped and bound in the decaying saloon. "What do you mean, beat it?" he said excitedly. "Don't you want out? Don't you see what they've done to you? Praise the Lord! Give me ten minutes and I'll have those chains off you."

The first man shifted around on his chair again, his feet making a clanking noise. He reached for his hip.

"Draw," he said.

Chris ducked back in the doorway as a shot rang out. He ran down the bridle path, stepping high with sore feet. Rounding a bend he suddenly came upon the ranch gate, and there parked outside it was the Mustang. He slowed his pace and reached for the keys, shaking his head.

Opening the car door, Chris found two men sitting in the back seat, smoking. One was about twenty-five and wore a tuxedo and black bow tie; the other was obviously a young hippie, beaded, hairy, with a fragrance on the ripe side.

"Well!" said Chris.

"Hello," said the man in the tux. "We're just hitchhikers."

"Hitchhikers to where?" asked Chris, wondering whether he should get in.

"Where are you heading?"

"I'm on my way to Life City."

The two in the rear seat grinned at each other. "That's where we want to go," said the young one.

Chris reacted pleasantly, then did a retake. "Did you walk down from the transmitter on the hill?" he asked.

They looked blank. "We must have bypassed it," said the one who had spoken first. "We came from Doomsdale by a shortcut."

Chris frowned. "I don't believe there is a shortcut," he said.

"What do you mean, there's no shortcut?" demanded the hippie. "You heard what he said—that's the way we came."

"It says in the book that no one gets in by shortcuts or back doors or any way except the main route and the front gate. I just read it on the hill. Don't you have a book?"

"Not with us," said the one in the tuxedo easily, "but we both have a wide acquaintance with the literature on the subject. Take formal prayer, for example. That's been my specialty at the seminary. I guess I've memorized a hundred prayers out of the old prayer books."

"Did anyone stamp your forehead?" asked Chris.

"Are you a nut or something?" asked the beaded one. "Even hippies don't stamp their foreheads."

"Well, fellows," said Chris, "I'd really like to take you, but there's no point in your going unless you have a passport."

"We have our credentials, old boy, don't worry," said the seminarian comfortably. "I've got a pass that will certify us through the gate."

"We're just as good as you are and don't you forget it!" said the hippie.

"You may be much better," said Chris, "but I don't think that cuts much ice in Life City. What you need is a briefing. There must be a way back to the transmitter from here. They can clue you in better than I can. Let me drop you off there."

"Oh, no you don't," said the hippie.

Chris tried another tack. "All right, let's go back up the trail to the top of the hill. That's where I got my passport. I'm sure they'll fix you up too." If there was one thing Chris did not feel like, it was another hike, but it was the only alternative.

"Why don't you just take us into Life City and forget all this skirmishing?" asked the tuxedoed one. "Doesn't the Word say, 'Whosoever will may come'?"

"I'm not clear about it," Chris admitted, "but I believe I was told at the transmitter that you have to come by the cross."

"Oh, I know all that. I've repeated it in church five thousand times. I believe it. What more do you want? Let's get moving."

Chris still hesitated. "I'll be glad to take you, but it doesn't seem right for you to waste—"

The hippie exploded. "This guy is weak. He turns me off," he snarled. "He won't take us along unless we've read the right books and repeated the right sayings. What's his bag anyway? No wonder the church is dead. Let's split out of here." He opened the door and got out.

The seminarian followed him and sighed as he held out his hand to Chris. "I think I would have enjoyed it," he said. "I might have been able to teach you some quaint old prayers along the way. But there is something about your theological position that repels me. It has too many *a priori's*. You apparently have no doctrine of the church—no sense of living tradition. Where, for example, do you work in the *leitourgia,* the *diakonia,* the *koinonia?* If going to Life City is as crass a thing as you make it out to be, I'm not sure I'm interested any more."

"Maybe we'll come and picket the place," said the hippie. "Have a croak-in."

Chris drove away, leaving the two doubled up in laughter.

Chapter 6

THE road, though not paved, was in good shape and the little Mustang sped through the rolling country-side at an easy clip; Chris was taking no more chances with side roads or detours. An occasional directional sign indicated that Life City lay ahead and Doomsdale behind; that was all he cared to know.

After a few hours of driving his body began to relax from the strain of the climb, and he grew sleepy. It was sundown when he reached the end of a long meadow and a road sign announced LOT'S WIFE MOTEL, 1/4 MILE. VACANCY. Crossing a bridge over a fast-moving stream, he swung the car into the driveway and parked in front of the office.

"Funny name you picked for your motel," he remarked to the manager, who had pink-rimmed blue eyes and rather long, pointed ears.

"I didn't pick it," was the reply.

"Who did?"

The manager pushed a registration card toward him. "It's

named for some formation or other back up the canyon. I never did bother to go look at it."

As Chris filled out the card he noticed the name at the top: *Lot's Wife Motel, Tim O'Rowse, prop. AAA. Public Restaurant. Rooms Payable in Advance. No Credit Cards or Personal Cheques.*

"Your name O'Rowse?" asked Chris holding out his hand. "Mine's Chris Anders."

"You just beat the rain," said the man solemnly. Chris decided that he looked like Dana's pet rabbit.

"Don't believe I've ever stayed here before."

"You on the road?"

"I was."

"We probably won't be here when you come through again."

"Why's that?"

"Oh, the new construction. It'll divert the traffic. Happened to me twice. You headin' through to Life City?"

"Yup."

"I doubt you can get up the grade, it's that bad. I wouldn't try it."

"Mr. O'Rowse," said Chris, "I'll tell you one thing, I'm not going back. Where's my room? And how are your steaks?"

The next morning Chris decided he would sleep in. He was tired, his legs were stiff, the bed was comfortable, it was raining, and it just seemed a good idea. By the time he finally got up, showered and breakfasted it was nearly noon. He presented his key at the office and found Mr. O'Rowse back on duty. The solemn blue eyes stared at him from their pink rims.

"You going to tackle it?" he asked.

"Why not?" asked Chris.

"It's raining bad."

"I know."

"There's a nineteen per cent uphill pull. It's pretty narrow, and the gravel is thin in spots. Probably be ruts by now."

"Probably."

"Well, if you're going," sighed O'Rowse, tugging at his ear, "be sure to keep on straight at the next intersection. They're doing construction on the crossroad and if you go to the right or left, you'll end in the ditch."

"OK."

"I heard on the radio there's cars right now stuck up there on Poopout Hill. I've seen 'em come backing all the way down."

"Look," said Chris, "this is the road to Life City, isn't it?"

"That's what they tell me."

"Then that's that. Good-bye, Mr. O'Rowse."

"Be careful."

As Chris turned back onto the road, he wondered why he felt so confident about this particular stretch of road, since he had known nothing but highway grief for two days. After some self-analysis he concluded it was because this time he was following orders. He thought about the passage he had read that morning in Isaiah: "They who wait for the Lord shall renew their strength, they shall mount up with wings like eagles, they shall run and not be weary, they shall walk and not faint." And he added to himself with a wry smile, "They shall drive and not miss their turns."

As he crossed the bridge it seemed to him that the stream had risen overnight. He reached the intersection, stopped for gas, then continued along a narrow gravel road that led steeply up Poopout Hill. He had climbed for about three miles when a huge puddle appeared in the road, and beyond it another, and another. He skidded the Mustang to a halt.

Well Brighteyes you've done it again Why didn't you get up before all this rain started You'd have been past all these puddles It would have been a breeze Now what do you do....

For several moments Chris stared disconsolately at the dripping elements. At length he thought of the verse in Isaiah, and reached around to pick up his Bible from the back seat. He was annoyed to discover it was not there. He swung around and searched the back of the seat, then the floor, then under the front seat. It did not take long to shatter his peace of mind completely. He got out in the rain, opened the trunk, and went through his suitcase. The Bible was nowhere to be found. Worn out by the effort and soaked, he got back in the car and tried to think.

I know I had that Bible this morning I know it I know it I read that passage lying on the bed Only thing I can think of it must be on that bedside table in Tim's motel This is fantastic come to think of it Why should I lose my cool over a book that forty-eight hours ago I couldn't have cared less about Why suddenly this lost feeling that has my skin crawling You'd think the Bible had some magic properties like Aladdin's lamp or some fool deodorant I don't understand it I can't argue with it I'm just going back that's all This thing is getting more important to me than life itself The Major called it a passport and a passport I gotta have, rain or no rain....

The road being extremely narrow, Chris was forced to back up the entire three miles, and narrowly missed the ditch on several occasions. He was worn out by the slow, arduous effort. Reaching the motel entrance at last, he hurried to his former room. There he found a cleaning dolly parked in the hall, the door ajar and a maid inside. He burst in, startling her so that she dropped the pillow she was changing.

"Sorry," he said, "I came back for my Bible. Have you seen it?"

"Seen what?"

"My Bible. I thought I left it on the bed table."

"They's nothin' here," she said. "I didn't see nothin'."

Chris stepped into the bathroom and back. "It's got to be here, unless I dropped it in the mud getting into the car." He began pulling open drawers in desperation. At the end of the built-in chest he jerked open the last drawer and shouted.

"It's here!" he said, drawing it out from under a Gideon Bible and a Book of Mormon. "Praise God. Oh, praise God!"

The maid came over to look. "A Bible," she said. "Man, I thought you said a bottle!"

"That was last month. Things have changed." He planted a kiss on the book's black cover. The maid stared at him wide-eyed.

"Now, what would a man like you be doin' with that Bible?" she asked.

"I just got saved, sister. The Lord made a new thing out of me. Aren't you saved?"

"Saved? Man, I'm saved, sanctified, baptized with the Holy Ghost an' with fire, but it ain't doin' me a stitch of good in this place. It takes more'n religion to keep body an' soul together when you workin' for that cat up front."

"What's wrong with him?"

"He jus' born wrong an' never quit!"

Chris wondered what he should say. "I guess the thing to do, sister, is to pray for him."

"No sir, I'm too busy prayin' at him an' against him. I believe the devil got a good thing goin' in Tim O'Rowse. He's somep'n else." She disappeared into the bathroom with the mop. Chris started for the door, then paused.

"Ma'am," he called out.

The maid poked her head around the corner of the wall.

"You-all talkin' to me?" she asked.

"Yes. Have you ever been to Life City?"

Something seemed to happen to her bearing as she groped for an answer. "I was there," she admitted softly, coming back into the room. Her face was expressionless.

"Did it—was it—" Chris gave up and waited for her to continue.

"They handed me an assignment," she said at last. "I fluffed it. Got mixed up with the wrong kind of folks."

"Maybe it's still not too late—" Chris ventured.

She shook her head. "It's way too late. He's dead. What I need to do is go back for a new set of orders, but I'm stuck."

"Why are you stuck? I'll give you a lift."

She looked at him and then out at the Mustang standing in the rain. Again she shook her head. "I told you it was too late."

Chris realized he had said the wrong thing and started to leave. At the door he turned. "Ma'am," he said, "forgive me for walking into your life, but if I were you I'd get out of here as fast as I could—today." He got back into his car and drove it past the office. Tim O'Rowse was standing inside the screen door watching him. Chris waved. The rain having stopped momentarily, the proprietor came out.

"I forgot to warn you," he said. "There's a big estate at the end of the thirty-mile stretch up yonder. It's just where you start to go down. Watch out for them big hounds they got loose up there. Keep your car windows up, or they'll jump right up and bite you."

"Did they do it to you?" asked Chris wonderingly.

"No, but I heard tell of it." He squinted at the rain, which had begun again. "Way it's comin' down, you're in for trouble. I wouldn't try it."

"Tim," said Chris, "have you ever made this trip to Life City?"

"Nope. Never have."

"Well, why don't you let somebody else take over and you come along and keep me company?"

"Oh, I guess I couldn't do that. Got this place to look after, and the help is terrible. I thought more'n once I'd like to go, but there always seems to be somethin' comes up. This mornin' you can see the creek is up three feet, and if it don't quit rainin' I'm sure the bridge will go out. But I'm obliged to you." He smiled glumly.

"Does a fellow named van Gelst ever come through here?" asked Chris.

"Oh sure, the Bible chap. You know him?"

"Yes, I do. What do you think of him?"

"Nice fellow. Real nice. Keeps nigglin' at me, but I don't give much. I kind of figure I'll make it one way or another."

"He gave me a good steer a while back."

"Oh, he's a fine lad."

"So long, Brother Tim," said Chris, holding out his hand. He drove out to the road and stopped on the shoulder to watch the creek water swirling at the piers of the bridge. He opened his Bible and found on the inside cover a printed list of "Scripture for Particular Needs." Running his finger down the list, he came to "When in Doubt About a Course of Action." The verse listed was Revelation 3:8, and he turned to it: "Behold, I have set before you an open door, which no one is able to shut." Chris slapped the book shut, grunted, and headed for Poopout Hill.

The next thirty miles were everything Tim O'Rowse said they were. He splashed through the puddles and crawled up the nineteen per cent grade. Here and there the gravel had been completely washed away, and some dangerous ruts had developed that nearly trapped the car. Twice he was forced to thread his way around an abandoned vehicle. Going over the first summit he found himself bouncing on a washboard road that nearly shook the fillings out of his teeth. Mile after mile it stretched, and the Mustang began to develop squeaks and rattles hitherto unknown. A squall struck the windshield with such force that for a while the wipers stopped working.

Still he kept inching along, humming "Turn It Over to Jesus" until the tune seemed to synchronize with the engine. To get it out of his mind he turned on the radio, which announced a special bulletin to the effect that the United States Government had responded to China's warning by mobilizing the National Guard and declaring a national emergency. The Civil Defense Administration had swung into action, and fallout shelters were again booming on the market. Chris turned off the set and began thinking about his family.

Here I am Lord safe secure delivered sealed and bound for Life City and there they are back there in that hole Seems like that's the way it's always been me here and they're someplace else Why is it I'm such a lousy father What's the matter with me Why didn't I ever pick up the boys when they were little and wanted to be picked up Seems as if I always had a deal going Look at Eileen and me living like two lodgers under the same roof for seven months while the temperature goes down down down down Flowers and golf and bridge I wish I could help her and the boys now I wish I could get them out of that place before it blows up But Ernie's right It's Life City now for me or devil take all Jesus are You going to take my family away from me Help me Lord They're all I've got except You I know it says something like loving You better than son or daughter or else we're not worthy but God I'm thinking of little Dana I can see him turning around in front of the TV and saying Where's Dad Can You understand me Lord What I mean is You saved me will You save my loved ones. . . .

Chris became aware that he had reached another summit. The rain had finally ceased and a late afternoon sun was trying to break through. The road had improved, and he rolled down his window to look at the imposing elm-lined drive he was entering. He passed through a gate which carried a brass plate reading PILGRIMS' MANOR HOUSE. ENTER. A hundred yards farther along he began to hear a furious barking and promptly rolled up the window. When he rounded a curve and came upon the two huge mastiffs that were making the noise, he was relieved to find them securely chained to stakes.

"O'Rowse was wrong again," he thought.

Farther on he came to a guard station with a cottage behind it. A man in uniform was standing in the road in the twilight, flashlight and clipboard in hand, waiting for him.

"Going on through?" he asked.

"Yes," said Chris, "but I'll never make it tonight. Is there any—"

"Your name, please."

"Christian Anders."

"Address?"

"Doomsdale. But I don't live there any more."

"Destination?"

"Life City. What's this for? Is this a state park or something?"

"No sir. This is Pilgrims' Manor House. It's owned and operated by the heirs of Lord Manson."

"Does this road belong to them?"

"Yes sir. The estate covers the whole top of the hill."

"Well, it's too dark now to try to make the descent. Any place here where they can put me up?"

"I believe so, sir, if you have been certified as a bona fide traveler to Life City." He held up his flashlight. "Would you mind my putting the amber beam on your face?"

"I guess not."

The guard scrutinized Chris' forehead quickly and then snapped off the light. "Thanks very much. I expect you have a passport."

"What kind of passport?"

"Did they give you a Bible?"

"Oh, yes. It's here in the front seat, but it happens to be my own Bible."

"Thank you, sir. That's all I want to know. I'm Captain Petrovich. If you'll just drive on up to the main door, I'll telephone ahead and they'll be waiting for you. Some of the girls will be able to tell you about the accommodations.

Good evening." The man turned and disappeared into the cottage. Chris drove on a quarter of a mile through the trees until he came to a stately Georgian mansion with white pillars fronting on a beautiful expanse of lawn. The entrance was flood-lit, and the early evening air was suddenly punctured by a burst of laughter as four teen-age girls came romping out the huge door. They caught sight of the Mustang and swarmed over it, exclaiming, "What a neat car! Let's take a ride! Whee! Let's go-go-go!"

One of them finally took notice of Chris and said, "Don't mind us, we just finished our work and feel good. How are you?"

"I'm fine," said Chris, "except for a few bird pecks on the head."

"The birds! I'm sorry," she said. "The devil's not really a very nice person, is he? My name's Char."

"How do you do. I'm Chris Anders. Do you suppose there's a cot out in the barn where I could sleep tonight?"

"Nothing of the sort," said one of the others, who had subsided somewhat. "You're a guest of the Manor. Captain Petrovich said so. We've already arranged to have you in the East Room."

"What's your name?"

"I'm Patty. And this is Pru and this is Creshie. And the chef wants to know if you would like steak and kidney pie."

"You tell the chef I'll take what's on his menu, all of it."

"Well, let's see," said Creshie, "there's worms and slugs and some fat lizards with tomato sauce—"

"Creshie," said Char, "I'm going to tell Uncle Gabe to change your name."

"Why?" asked Chris, amused.

"Because she was named Discretion and she's anything but. If she didn't love the Lord—"

"Discretion! What a monicker. How do you survive it?"

Creshie giggled. "Anybody who calls me Discretion gets short-sheeted. But really, it's no worse than theirs. Her name isn't Patty, it's Piety. And she's Prudence and she's Charity."

By this time Chris had taken his bags out of the car and they were leading him into the house. He was escorted to a handsome upper room with an eastern view overlooking the valley. After washing up and soothing his several wounds he came down the winding staircase to the ornate drawing room, where hors d'oeuvres and soft drinks awaited him. One by one the girls came in, attractively dressed for dinner. They served him and sat down. Chris was struck by the well-groomed look of their faces and the modesty of their bearing as much as by the zest they seemed to draw from life.

"While we're waiting for supper," said Char, "we want to hear something about your adventures."

"What would you like to know?" Chris was suddenly feeling very mellow indeed.

"About the birds," said Creshie. "The horrid things. I'm so glad ours are nice." She whistled shrilly, and a parakeet came flying in to light on her shoulder.

"Creshie," said Char, "you know we don't whistle around here after sundown."

"Excuse me, Mr. Anders," said Creshie. "We do want to hear about Doomsdale."

"All I can tell you is that I got out."

"But how did you know where to go?"

"Why, I bumped into Ernie van Gelst. Do you know him?"

"Bless his heart," said Pru, "of course we know him. He

stayed here two nights ago. We're doing Bible study in the Book of Acts together."

"Well, he told me how to get to the transmitter. I didn't take the direct route, but we won't go into that. I did manage to meet the Colonel and the Major, and they put me through the business."

"Don't you just love Major Putter?" asked Patty. "I think he's darling. That funny little mustache."

"What do you mean by the business?" asked Char.

"Oh, that film. People trying to put the fire out, and that poor devil trapped in the Château d'If. Frankly, it scared me."

"You didn't see the other one?"

"About the end of the world? No, I told the Major I couldn't take any more. I guess he thought I was pretty well saturated, because he turned me loose."

"Was that when you ran into the birds?" asked Creshie, making faces at her parakeet, who responded raucously in kind.

"I told you, Creshie, not to try to put that budgie's head in your mouth," Char rebuked her.

"Sorry," murmured Creshie, giving the parakeet a very stern look.

"When did your back trouble start?" Char asked of Chris.

"I was reading the New Testament one night—in the Book of Revelation—and I felt this burning sensation. They must have known about it in the Principality, because they hit me with a UFO right on the upper spine. I thought I was done for. Then they sent the birds; but it came out all right."

"Do you know what that pain was?" inquired Char.

"I guess you'd better tell me," replied Chris.

"It was the burden of your sin, Mr. Anders. The passage

you read in Revelation simply made you aware of it. The problem was there all the time."

"And here I thought it was someplace else," murmured Chris.

"Like in Moscow, maybe?" suggested Creshie, her eyes twinkling.

"Or in Peking. Or—in my kids."

"Then what happened after that?" asked Pru.

"Then I went up the skull face and got saved. And the pain went away. Just like that."

The girls looked at him seriously for a second and then burst into oh's and ah's and clapped their hands.

"What's your first name, Mr. Anders?" asked Creshie.

"Christian. They call me Chris."

She started singing softly. Patty picked up a guitar and the others joined in harmony:

> Hallelujah! 'tis done!
> Chris believes on the Son,
> He's saved by the blood
> Of the Crucified One.

Their voices were young and true. When they finished Patty asked, "Did they stamp you on your forehead? And give you those nice outdoor clothes you're wearing?"

"Yes, they did. Three hikers came up, stripped to the waist and covered with grease, and carrying packs. It was perfect timing. So then I went down the hill and got shot at by some old coot of a gambler."

"That must have been the Lazy 3," said Char.

"I wondered who they were."

"Oh, they've been there for years. I think they originally

started out to climb the hill, but they took up ranching instead. One night someone from the Principality of Belial sneaked in and chained them while they were asleep at the card table. They had been drinking a lot, I'm afraid."

"Go on," said Pru. "What happened then?"

"Why, I found my car with two hitchhikers sitting in it. They were a strange combination. One was a theological student dressed in a tuxedo and the other was a hippie."

"We know about them," piped up Creshie.

"They told me they were taking a shortcut to Life City, and wanted a lift."

"I used to date that student before I met Christ," said Char. "He has the strangest notions about religion. He likes all the trappings but won't have anything to do with the real thing."

"That's why he wears the tux," explained Patty. "He likes to go formal."

"Did you ever date the other guy?" grinned Chris.

Char blushed. "You mean the hippie? We don't really know him. He's a—"

"Hypocrite," Patty interrupted. "He isn't even a true hippie—just a gross character. I can't imagine why he wants to go to Life City."

"Probably he just likes to take trips," said Creshie to her parakeet. Pru rose and excused herself from the room.

"Are you married, Mr. Anders?" asked Char.

"Very much so," said Chris. "I left a wife and four boys in Doomsdale."

"Why didn't you bring them with you?" asked Creshie. "Wasn't the car big enough?"

"It wasn't that," said Chris. "They wouldn't come." The

conversation then turned to the girls, and they shared some of their experiences as hostesses at the Manor House. Presently they took him into a parlor that had been turned into a museum. Here Lord Manson had gathered a magnificent Bible collection. In addition to fragments of early manuscripts, they showed him the Bible William Carey had translated at Serampore in India, and Adoniram Judson's first Burmese Bible, Robert Morrison's Chinese Bible, Henry Martyn's Persian text, and many others. They explained that their tour of duty at the Manor would end pretty soon; they would be replaced by another crew from Life City and would be reporting for fresh orders. Meanwhile they provided hospitality and encouragement for all travelers on that road.

"You sure do a nice job," was Chris' reaction.

At this point Pru returned and announced, "Dinner is being served. Mr. Anders, Lord Manson would like you to come and meet some other members of his family."

Chapter 7

THE following morning Chris breakfasted royally on poached eggs and link sausages and was exposed to a thoughtful reading of the fifteenth chapter of Luke and given a tour of the rest of the Manor House by some of the staff. He then made ready to leave. The girls provided him with a surprise going-away present: a flight bag containing his clean linen, freshly ironed, and a lunchbasket full of delicacies suited to masculine taste. Captain Petrovich brought the Mustang around to the door, serviced, washed and ready to roll. Chris took the four sisters on a spin through the grounds, during which they taught him another Gospel chorus:

> I have decided to follow Jesus,
> No turning back, no turning back. . . .
> The cross behind me, the crown before me,
> No turning back, no turning back.

After listening to the soft, young voices, he found making his farewells rather difficult. "I've really never met people quite like you," he said, misty-eyed. "It doesn't seem possible for folks to be so happy down inside. But if that's what Christ does, I want in. Thank you for what you've taught me."

"But you've been so nice!" exclaimed Creshie.

"Nothing special about us," said Patty. "We put up our hair every night. But we think being Christians is the greatest fun there is."

"And we're going to pray about your family," added Pru.

"Please do," said Chris, with tears now frankly running down his face. "I wish—I wish my boys could—" He paused and blew his nose. Char said nothing, but going up to him pinned a button to the inside of his wool shirt collar.

"What's it say?" sniffed Chris, trying to read it.

"All-prayer," she said quietly.

"All-prayer? What's that?"

"It's in the sixth of Ephesians, Mr. Anders. All-prayer is prayer in the Spirit."

"It just means all-out," put in Creshie. "Tells it like it is!"

"Well!" murmured Chris.

"Now that you're a Christian, you're going to need it," said Char. "We don't know what's waiting for you down there in Prone Valley, but we have an idea."

"Did you say Prune Valley?"

"Prone Valley."

"Named after a Mr. Prone," said Patty.

"Who's that?"

"You!" Their laughter bubbled up again.

"Mr. van Gelst says it's where all the spare tires go flat," said Creshie, sending them off into another peal.

Puzzled but in a very good humor, Chris started the engine,

and after handshakes all around he drove out past the guard post. "God in your heart!" they called, waving him out of sight. He began the winding descent and within half an hour the Mustang reached the valley floor, which he found to be stony, dry and desolate. The roadbed was narrower than ever and in an advanced state of neglect. It was evident that the valley was a giant rock wash. Boulders hemmed in the traveler on either side, making it virtually impossible for two cars to pass. Once Chris spotted a weathered, teetering signpost with the faint lettering LIFE CITY and an arrow pointing in the direction he was going. Otherwise he could see no indication of life. He might as well have been driving in a moon crater.

After six or seven miles his eye was caught by some kind of object on the road in the distance. At first he thought it was stationary, but as he drove nearer he found it to be a huge bulldozer that was apparently pushing some rock fill into a ditch alongside the road. The heavy equipment was squarely across the right of way. Stopping the Mustang some yards off, Chris got out and began walking toward the dozer. His thumb felt for the button on his collar.

"All-prayer," he said, feeling uneasy.

The operator of the bulldozer brought it to a clanking halt. As he stepped down Chris noticed some black lettering on the huge blade. Someone had crudely painted the words, CARTHAGE, TOLEDO, DROGHEDA, LIDICE, AUSCHWITZ and other place names. Now the man advanced half a dozen paces toward him, and it came over Chris that his face was familiar. He was a heavy type, weighing perhaps two hundred pounds and standing slightly under six feet. His clothing consisted of a greasy T-shirt with the faded letters *B* and *L* on the chest, and a pair of black dungarees. There was something odd to Chris about the way the man's eyebrows pointed to his nose. The thick, sensual mouth opened and he spoke.

"Where do you think you're goin'?" he asked.

"Life City," said Chris, a bit shaken by the ugly tones in the man's voice.

"Yeah? Where you from?"

"Doomsdale."

"Doomsdale!" He swore a crude oath. "That's my territory. I operate all that section."

"You do?" Chris felt his knees buckle forward. "What's your name?"

"Never mind." The man reached for a quid of tobacco. "I know you, you're one of my boys."

"I—?"

"What's buggin' you? Eh? Why you wanna leave Doomsdale? Doncha like workin' for me?"

Chris swallowed. "I didn't know I was. Maybe that explains—" He didn't finish. He was thinking about Eileen and the boys, trapped in a community that was subservient to something like this.

The thick lips managed a smile. "I just don't like folks leavin' my territory," he said.

Chris decided he could not afford to let his fear show. "I'm already signed up," he announced.

"Signed up with wot?"

"I'm a Christian."

The smile grew broader and became tangled in teeth. "Don't let it bother you," he said. "I run across you guys all the time. You leave for a while, but you come driftin' back."

"Not me."

The man spat a stream and put his fists on his hips. "Why not? I'm not hard to get along with. I let bygones be bygones."

"I'm not switching," Chris insisted shakily.

"OK, OK, you asked for it. If you wanna spend the rest of your days bein' a fake, go ahead. I want honest men who know what they are and don't muss with all this religious trash."

"You've got me wrong," said Chris.

"Like so much bull. I got you dead to rights, big boy."

Chris felt his pockets. He was not carrying even a jackknife. The operator wiped his nose with a greasy forearm. "Lookatcha," he went on derisively. "Goin' to Life City. What's your bag? Think they want you there? You spent more time off the road than you did on it, what I hear. You went and lost your passport. An' what about your wife and kids? You think the man'll give you a medal for walkin' out on 'em?"

Chris hung his head. "It's all true," he said.

"I heard you got to messin' around those fillies at the Manor last night. I know what you were thinkin', you liar! You pass yourself off in front of them as bein' so brave and strong, and such a holy Joe, when all you want is you know what. Oh, you're a real piece, you are. The holy pilgrim! John Bunyan rides again! But I know better."

"Keep going," said Chris.

"Why should I?"

"Because everything you said is true, and there's a lot more. You've got your man taped—I'm a stinker and don't deny it." Chris took his hands from his pockets, raised his head and looked his adversary in the eye. "What you don't

know is that it's all covered by the blood over there on that
hill." Chris pointed in the direction from which he had
come.

The operator spat again, and an ugly look spread over his
features. "I don't like that kind of chicken talk," he said.
"Where I run things, a joker pays up for what he done. He
don't pass the buck to nobody. But then, I turn out *men!*"
He came closer to Chris. "Did I hear you say you were a
Christer?" Chris did not reply; he simply watched the man's
eyes. Suddenly a huge hand came up and smote him heavily
on the cheek. Reeling back, he barely managed to keep his
balance. "OK, Christer," growled the operator, "let's have
the other side, like it says." Chris stayed where he was. "Not
gonna play Bible games, eh? Don't like the way the man sets
it out when it comes down to the nitty gritty, do ya?"

"Are you going to let me pass?" Chris demanded.

The man swung around. "Sure I will," he said, "but first
I'm gonna fix your cute lil wagon."

He turned again toward the dozer. Chris looked at the
Mustang and decided he had about two seconds in which to
act. It was not an easy decision. As a computer salesman he
had not kept himself in the best of physical condition. There
was a telltale bulge under his belt. He stood perhaps two
inches shorter and weighed thirty pounds less than this man.
His competitive athletics had been high school football,
farther back than he cared to remember. Four weeks ago he
had played nine holes of golf. That was it.

Nevertheless Chris bolted forward, left his feet, and struck
the man amidships. Down they went, crashing into the push
arm of the bulldozer. Chris caught a whiff of the same sicken-
ing odor he had smelled in the creek where he first got stuck,

and on the trail down from the transmitter. He recovered quickly and backed away, for the man had pulled a large crescent wrench out of his rear pocket and was now advancing menacingly. His appearance was frightening; blood—or was it blood?—streamed down one ear from the wound where his head had struck the dozer.

"Why don't you let me pass?" Chris cried out in terror. "I haven't done you any harm. What have you got against me?"

The man's lips parted in what should have been a smile. He touched his free hand to his ear and looked at it. "No harm!" he said. "C'mere, baby. Don't go 'way like that. Just c'mere."

Chris ran around behind the Mustang. "You want to kill me," he shouted. "You want to—!" He thought of the three men he had met on the summit of Skull Hill. One had given him his Bible; that was lying in the car. One had given him clothes. What had the other done? He couldn't remember, but suddenly it seemed terribly important. What was it? He dodged around to the other side of the car as the man came relentlessly after him. What was it? What was it? His forehead! No wonder he couldn't remember. He put his hand to it, and there came to him the prayer he had uttered in desperation on the transmitter hill. "God!" he cried again. "Neutralize!"

He noticed the aerial on his Mustang; it gleamed in the noonday sun perhaps a bit more brightly than usual. Working his way around, keeping his opponent blocked, he got to the aerial and with a violent wrench snapped it off. As he did so he was staggered and forced back by a crushing blow on his left shoulder. The wrench had come flying across the hood, knocking him off his feet and sending the aerial spinning into the dirt. Like a cat the big man was around the car and upon him, and over they rolled, the greasy T-shirt in Chris' face and thick fingers tightening on his throat. Now the huge frame had him pinned; Chris' left arm was caught in a hammerlock and he felt something it in snap; the fingers had left his throat and were pressing his eyes into their sockets, while a forearm was jammed against his windpipe. All the breath had left his lungs. His eyes were lumps of sheer pain. Hope left him; prayer left him; there was nothing but evil. In that instant, just before consciousness faded, his free hand found the steel rod in the dirt beside him. He grasped it and feebly pointed the broken end against the skin of his opponent.

With a mighty curse the man leaped off his prey, got unsteadily to his feet and began scratching his shirt. Chris rolled over onto his knees, shook his head and blinked, trying to see. His left arm hung limp. After a second or two, during which the operator emitted a series of vile caterwaulings, things came back together; before his adversary returned to the attack Chris had managed to stagger to his feet and reach the other side of the Mustang. Another two seconds of recovery and his brain began working at survival speed. Clinging to the aerial, he decided that the key to the outcome was the bulldozer. Maneuvering to the front of the Mustang, he made a dash for the big machine.

With a blood-freezing yell the operator came in pursuit —he had picked up the wrench. Chris darted to the rear of the bulldozer and found himself in a roadbed cluttered with rocks and dirt fill. The ditch alongside was perhaps two hundred feet in length and nearly filled. What lay underneath he could only guess, but the long trench gave off a smell of death and putrefaction that made his stomach turn over. What kind of monster was this? He turned and found that the man had mounted into the driver's seat and started up the equipment. The dozer was now bearing down on his precious car with obvious intent to crush it on the rocks at the side of the road.

Dizzy from his latest affliction, Chris leaped on the moving vehicle and scrambled up toward the operator, aerial in hand. The dozer was now advancing at full speed on its target. The driver turned, saw Chris and hurled the wrench, which just grazed his ear. Chris then reached around and lanced the man lightly between the shoulder blades. He yelled, threw up his hands and leaped, with Chris following nimbly after him. The bulldozer proceeded to career wildly off the road, missing the Mustang by inches and piling into a nest of boulders, where it stalled.

Once again the two men were on the road; once again they were confronting each other, but this time it was Chris who did the advancing, steel whip in hand, while his assailant retreated and tried to scratch his back. Never had Chris heard such execrable indecencies as now proceeded from his lips. As they circled, each watching for an opening, the man's hand left his back and Chris became convinced of what he feared: that the stunning effect of the aerial was only temporary. This enemy had powers of recuperation beyond those of ordinary flesh and blood. He studied the faded lettering on the T-shirt until he made out the full word: BELIAL.

Now Chris began to realize the nature of his struggle. Here he was at the end of his strength, pitted against a man who could not tire. The measure of fatigue was the measure of the battle. Something frothed in his mouth, and he wiped his lips on the collar of his jacket, then felt a prick on his thumb —it was the button Char had pinned on him. "All-prayer," he thought. "Tells it like it is." He took a step forward, brandishing the aerial, but before he could speak his prayer Belial backed into a large stone on the side of the road and tripped. As he toppled in the dirt roaring with rage, Chris rushed up to him and, bending over, touched the lance to his heart. The bellowing stopped. Chris telescoped the aerial and tucked it under his limp left arm. With his good arm he propelled the stone over on top of his adversary. Then he rolled up a second large stone and settled it on the inert body. Then another and another, until the figure was completely covered.

Stumbling back to the bulldozer, Chris climbed into the seat and began with one hand frantically working the steering controls. Soon he had the engine idling. A few false moves and he had the dozer backed onto the road, where he swung it about and, working the hoist control, moved the blade toward the pile of rocks. Scraping the pile off the road and into the ditch, he then gunned the bulldozer until its crawler track stopped on top of the fill, leaving the road clear. Somewhere underneath was the fiend Belial, recovering once more, Chris suspected, from the effect of the steel lance.

Chris jumped clear of the equipment and scrambled up and out of the smelly ditch. As he did so he dislodged a partially covered foot bone which seemed to him unmistakably human. His fears were now fairly confirmed: the ditch was nothing but a mass grave. Panting, he ran back to his own vehicle and turned over the engine. He picked his way carefully past the loose rocks still on the road, and once clear of the scene, noting no signs of life in the rearview mirror, he gave a great shudder and opened the throttle.

Take me out of here baby Oh get me out of here I've never been so scared in my life There must be hundreds of bodies rotting under there but he didn't get me Just my shoulder and arm Well they'll heal Maybe it's not a break after all What in the world was in that aerial anyway Looks harmless enough now but I sure saw it glowing before and did it ever make him jump and scratch Old Scratch isn't that what they call him I've heard it somewhere I bet he's wriggling under that bulldozer right now trying to get out Let's go baby go go go Let's vacate this Prone Valley where all the spare tires go flat Yes sweetheart but it's also where the aerial of a Mustang suddenly becomes Excalibur the rapier of the Lord How about that Lord You made Your point Not even the devil can stand up to the sword of Your Spirit Nyaaaaa to all you demons in hell I'm gonna turn it over to Jesus yes and s-m-i-l-e the rest of the day. . . .

Chapter 8

THE Mustang reached the lower end of the rock wash without meeting further obstruction and wound its way into a low-lying range of hills. Topping a rise, it began the gradual descent into a sandy stretch. The character of the landscape changed again, this time to desert. The road became little more than an Indian track meandering amid sparse clumps of sage and mesquite. Apart from the desert vegetation and an occasional high-flying buzzard, signs of life were absent. Peculiar rock formations appeared and disappeared in the distance. The temperature rose until it seemed to Chris it could not possibly get any hotter. Treacherous sandy shoulders threatened to trap him the moment he became unwary at the wheel.

Stopping the car, Chris reached into the lunchbasket and broke out some cool lemonade from a thermos. He then switched on the radio to get his mind off the heat and the pain in his arm. Nothing happened. Then he remembered the broken aerial and, getting out, dug a small transistor radio from his suitcase. A newscaster was saying,

". . . and the first atomic warhead is expected to be fired within hours from an ICBM complex near Swatow. The United States anti-ballistic missile system has been activated and the Strategic Air Command has been placed on red alert by direct order of the President. National Guard troops are being assembled in metropolitan staging areas, in anticipation of a Congressional declaration of martial law. A Soviet delegation is flying to the United Nations. On the local scene, a flash flood racing out of the Diablo Range last night turned Eschaton Creek into a river of death that claimed the lives of an estimated sixteen persons staying at the Lot's Wife Motel. According to Weather Bureau officials, two inches of rain fell within sixty minutes between nine and ten P.M. By midnight the creek overflowed its banks. Flood waters smashed into the twelve-unit motel and turned the buildings into matchwood. Rescue workers are continuing to hunt for bodies amid the debris, but because of continuing flood conditions it is expected to be days before the count is completed. The one survivor of the disaster, Mrs. Arlowene Jackson, told a WEAL reporter she had been warned by God the day before to 'get out' of the motel. She said that last night when her ride failed to show up in the rain, she began walking to get away from the site, and had reached a point two miles downstream known as Ebenezer Hill when the creek waters began to rise. She took refuge in an abandoned hamburger stand. At the time she was picked up by a helicopter rescue team, it was learned, Mrs. Jackson was carrying the only thing left of the motel, a Gideon Bible she said she had taken from one of the rooms. . . ."

A car was approaching in the distance. Chris started the Mustang and began looking for a section of the road where it would not be dangerous to pass. He found a stretch near a clump of yuccas that seemed crustier than the rest, and eased the wheels onto the shoulder. The oncoming vehicle proved to be a battered convertible containing two persons. A sprung A-frame and a caved-in hood gave it the appearance of sashaying down the road. As it drew abreast Chris flagged down the driver.

"What happened to you?" he asked.

The driver peered at him through sunglasses. "We've had it," he said, working his mouth.

"Where're you heading?"

"Back."

"What do you mean, back?"

"He means," said the rider, who appeared younger and had a deeply sunburned face, "that we're not goin' the way you're goin'."

"We been there," agreed the driver. Apparently it was a nose tic that caused the mouth to work.

"What's ahead?" Chris asked.

"If we told you," said the sunburned one, "you wouldn't believe it."

"Isn't that the way to Life City?" Chris persisted.

"They told us it was," said the driver, "but we decided we ain't goin'. We'll settle for something else."

"Uncle Al's right," said the young man. "It's not worth it."

The driver took off his sunglasses and peered at Chris. "Who messed you up?" he asked.

Chris looked down at his limp arm. "Our friend back there," he said.

"On the bulldozer?"

"Yup."

"That was Belial," nodded the driver, twitching his nose.

"He gave us some trouble, too. But we're gonna go back and try to make a deal with him."

"You just might," said Chris, wondering whether the bulldozer was still in the ditch. "How far do you think you'll get today?"

"We figure to make Lot's Wife Motel by tonight," was the reply. "My cousin Tim there'll put us up and we can get this frame straightened out."

"Hey, how'd you lose your aerial?" the nephew wanted to know.

"I didn't." Chris lifted it from the seat beside him and held it up to view. Then he added, "If I were you I wouldn't try to reach the motel by tonight."

"Why not?" The driver put on his sunglasses.

"Well, because it's—" Chris swallowed, wondered how much he should say. "And stay away from Belial," he went on. "Look, I—I don't know how to talk about God—I feel like a fool—but you fellows are sure heading in the wrong direction. I mean, won't you turn around and go on with me? We'll make out. I'm sure we will."

The nose jerked. So did the convertible. "It's all yours," said the driver as he pulled ahead. The young man waved as they went swaying down the road in a cloud of sandy dust.

Discouraged by this fresh evidence of his lack of persuasive powers, Chris drove on, wondering if it meant he could no longer sell computers. He speculated on the kind of treatment that could twist a new car frame so badly out of line. The Mustang had progressed two or three miles when he came to a queer rock formation that projected out of the desert floor some three or four hundred feet. Parked in the shade of the rock he discerned a familiar object: a dusty black

Chevelle. And sitting alongside, clad in sport shirt and Bermudas and listening to a short-wave radio, was none other than E. van Gelst.

"Ernie!" cried Chris, getting out and going up to him with outstretched hand. "Isn't this a little off your run?"

Van Gelst half-rose to his feet for the greeting, then sank back and continued munching a lettuce sandwich. "No place is off my run," he said.

"Well, this time you found me on the right road, anyway."

Van Gelst nodded. "How's your arm?" he asked.

"Not very good. The shoulder bruise seems to be better, but I think that Belial snapped a bone above the elbow."

Van Gelst continued to eat. After he had finished his sandwich and had taken a drink of iced tea from his lunch box, he stood up and felt Chris' arm. "Take off your shirt," he said. Then, "I don't think it's a bone. Feels more like a pulled tendon." Walking over to his car, he took a small bottle from the glove compartment.

"What's that?" Chris inquired dubiously.

"Some ointment the wife cooks up. Myrtle leaves. I think she calls it Twenty-two-two."

"How come?" Chris wanted to know, as van Gelst rubbed his upper arm gently.

"I don't know. Something in Revelation, I guess." He finished and screwed the cap back on the bottle. "You see that sign on the rock?"

Chris walked around a point of the rock formation in the direction van Gelst was pointing. A sign had been daubed on a flat surface, VALLEY OF THE SHADOW OF DEATH.

"That what they call it?" Chris asked, thinking about the smashed convertible.

Van Gelst nodded. "Why don't you relax now and eat your lunch while I explain some things to you." They settled against the rock face and the man took a notebook from his hip pocket. "You see, you're about to drive through a magnetic field that extends roughly for the next fifty miles. Terrainwise, it won't seem any different from what you're now in, except that you'll pick up a paved road down here a ways; but for an hour or more you'll be exposed to a different kind of attack. In this one the target will be not your body, but your mind."

"My mind is in worse shape than my body is," reflected Chris. "I haven't read a book in eighteen months."

"Well, this is a kind of psychological—or perhaps I should say metaphysical—exposure," said van Gelst. "It'll come through your car radio."

"Oh no, it won't," said Chris. "I broke the aerial."

Van Gelst shook his head. "That won't stop it," he said. "Neither will your switch. I told you this was a metaphysical attack. It's being launched from a communications control center by the prince of the power of the air."

"Suppose I just turn up my transistor and drown him out."

"It won't work. In this magnetic field he'll come right through your transistor. In fact, there is only one weapon that will stop him."

"What's that?"

"A Scripture verse."

"Huh?"

Van Gelst took from his side pocket a small object. "This is a memory verse packet," he said, tossing it in his hand. "You'll find Bible verses lined up in a particular sequence. Now here's what to do. Set this packet on top of your dashboard, and every time you get a message on the radio, turn to the next verse and read it aloud. Read it twice. Get it in your head."

"You're not serious, Ernie."

"You'll find out how serious I am."

"But this is Sunday School stuff. 'Now I lay me down to sleep, I pray the Lord my soul to keep.' "

"That's not a Bible verse."

"Do I get a gold star anyway?"

Van Gelst leaned so close that Chris edged away from his eyeballs. "Anders," he said, "I've been informed there's a bulldozer back down the line heading this way. It has already pushed that sprung convertible into a ditch. Now do you want this packet or don't you?"

Chris took the packet.

While he finished eating he asked van Gelst to fill him in on a number of matters that had occupied his mind during his travels. He learned, first of all, that his own family was surviving well; that the boys were digging a fallout shelter in the back yard; that his wife Eileen was convinced he was dead and had gone to a seance hoping to establish some kind of contact with him but had been disappointed. He learned further that O. B. Stennett had had to give up golf and was under a doctor's care for overstrain, and that Warren Clay had seemed rather depressed since he returned from Stuck Creek. Guy Wise had been placed in a nursing home with liver and pancreas ailments. Colonel Goodall had been rotated back to Life City from the transmitter, and his place had been taken by Major Putter. The three hikers Chris had met on Gordon's Calvary van Gelst believed had been transferred to a helicopter rescue mission detail. As for the two hitchhikers, one, the hippie, was being held in the Carnapolis jail for robbery, while the other had disappeared. The men at the Lazy 3 Ranch were, as far as he knew, still playing cards and still chained.

"I got the word about Tim O'Rowse's motel on the radio," said Chris. "I was real sorry about that. I sort of liked old Tim."

"I know you spoke to Tim about coming with you," said van Gelst. "I tried to reach him many times. Something must have happened way back to turn him against the Lord. His heart was shut tight."

"They said there was a woman who got out," said Chris. "A maid. I think I knew her."

"I should say you did. You gave her the word that saved her life."

"What do you mean?"

"I mean she's on her way back to Life City right now. Staying with the girls at the Manor House, I believe."

"You've got to be kidding."

"I never kid anyone, Anders. She has a story to tell and she's telling it."

A remote but ominous clanking noise began to be heard on the road. Chris jumped to his feet in alarm.

"Is that guy going to trail me the rest of my life?" he demanded.

Van Gelst shook his head. "Belial won't enter the magnetic field if he can avoid it," he said. "It belongs to another Principality, and they're usually not very friendly toward each other. Evil, as you know, is divisive. But perhaps you'd better get going."

Chris held up the packet in his left hand. "This little light o' mine," he sang, "I'm gonna let it shine."

"Your arm feel better now?" asked van Gelst.

Chris stopped in the middle of a note, his mouth open, and felt the spot above his elbow. The pain had disappeared. "Hey," he said. But van Gelst was already getting into his car. Chris ran over to him, words of gratitude tumbling over each other as he tried to speak. The other man said nothing, but pointed at a dark object far down the road. Chris hurried back to the Mustang and started it; but before he put it into gear he took time to look up Revelation 22:2 in his Bible: "Also, on either side of the river, the tree of life with its twelve kinds of fruit, yielding its fruit each month; and the leaves of the tree were for the healing of the nations."

Chris sailed down the road and into the next Principality.

Chapter 9

"WELCOME to the Principality of Beelzebul, the Lord of the Flies. As you travel through these invisible precincts sacred to demonry, we shall present for your edification such instruction as will heighten your appreciation of human culture and your understanding of the aspirations of all people. First, a word about demons. There is a good deal of misinformation in the common folklore with regard to demons. Many think of us as imps, or gnomes, or wicked little gremlins that hide in the woodwork or jump in and out of people. This is a travesty. The truth is that demons are nothing more than ideas. We are the impulses of reason and intelligence, dedicated to the building of a universe operated by man's scientific thought and rational control. We hope that during this time together you will get to like us.

"One of the surest signs of the emancipation of man from the darkness of ignorance has been his willingness to examine the basis of his religious convictions. The learner will soon discover, if he is truly objective, that all such beliefs are based upon primitive superstitions. These superstitions, all of which are born out of fear and dread, can be found even today among tribespeople in the remote sectors of human habitation.

"Primitive man, prehistoric man, as we know from archaeological evidence, instinctively attributed the events that surrounded
his daily life to the intervention of supernatural powers. Thus
every tree had its god; every stream had its spirit; every hilltop
had its sacred ring where something or other was worshiped. With
the coming of the age of science, of course, all such simple
credulities have been dissolved. The light of knowledge has driven
out the darkness of belief. It is no longer possible for modern
man, educated in the heritage of human culture and trained in
the physical and social sciences, to hold to the existence of the supernatural. We shall continue after a brief pause for station identification. You are listening to Radio WARP in Beelzebul. . . ." *ha.*

*You know I don't like to admit it but this man has got
something How can I question science It's all right to believe
in God but the fact is I've never seen him The preachers
have never seen him The astronauts have never seen him
And the fellow's right this spook business is for the birds
When you look at the universe it's obvious that it operates
along certain principles When you look at people they react
according to pattern Like if I meet a customer who needs
help and I make a good pitch I sell a computer It's just as
simple as that Where does the religion come in Anyway here
I am driving along this road and heading for a place called
Life City that's supposed to be full of holy Joes To be honest
I don't know that there is any such place I've gone and left* ef 9u(2
*a place I know for a place I don't know Why Who knows
I suppose because of Ernie but who's Ernie Well he's somebody who says when I hear something on the radio I'm supposed to read a Bible verse OK Ernie here's your Bible verse
"Ever since the creation of the world his invisible nature
namely his eternal power and deity has been clearly per-
ceived in the things that have been made So they are without*

excuse" Hey that sounds pretty good I'm going to run through it again Wait a minute What's happening to the radio There's a lot of interference coming from some place Must be the broken aerial Let's see if I can figure out what this verse means It says there's a God all right and only a fool could ignore the evidence that we see all around us Well I never did disbelieve really I just. . . .

"Station WARP wishes to make apology for the transmission difficulty that momentarily interrupted our program. Continuing our presentation of modern man and the demonic, we would like to draw your attention to the scientific progress being made in recent New Testament studies. For the past twenty years the key word has been 'demythologize.' Now, demythologizing the New Testament—or the Old, for that matter—means simply removing from it those portions (there are many of them, we regret to say) which are unacceptable to the modern human intelligence. You see, the trained intellect will want to examine such things as miracle stories from a different frame of reference than that of a medieval monk, let us say, or a woodcutter in the Black Forest.

"Now, to eliminate miracle is not to weaken the New Testament or to render it historically less important. On the contrary, demythologizing greatly enhances the importance of the ancient documents. It renders them scientifically reliable—to a degree. For example, the four Gospels frequently refer to Jesus as the 'Son of God.' John, the so-called author of the Fourth Gospel, is the worst offender in this respect. But 'Son of God' is a purely mythological term. We find it in the myth heritage of Egypt, of Babylon, of Assyria, of Greece, of Rome, of all the ancient cultures. To modern man it is an expression that means nothing.

"When we strip Jesus of this title we see him immediately as he really was, a provincial Jewish religious leader who borrowed most of his ideas from earlier rabbis. We discover that it was his followers who built him up into a supernatural figure after his death. These followers invented the term 'Son of God' in order to aggrandize their own importance. They also introduced the stories of his virgin birth and his rising from the dead in order to create a basis for the new religious establishment they hoped to erect. . . ."

Isn't that something I always suspected these things but I could never put them into words Now if I could see a miracle happening right before my eyes I might be impressed Like if this Mustang were to turn into a Cadillac I'd say that would be a miracle But I don't know about a woman having a baby without a man around And there was always something that bothered me too about what happened to the body of Jesus I never mentioned it but I wish somebody would explain it to me about the cells decomposing and recomposing and all that business Maybe this guy is right we just have to demythol—whatever it is get Jesus down where we are so we can understand him I don't see why the New Testament shouldn't be studied scientifically like anything else except old Ernie of course He won't like that He just thinks take another Bible verse and that will settle everything Well what is the next Bible verse Ernie "If you confess with your lips that Jesus is Lord and believe in your heart that God raised him from the dead you will be saved" Now that doesn't say anything about myths or science I'm just going to take another look at it "If you confess with your lips that Jesus is Lord and believe in your heart that God raised him from the dead you will be saved" Hello the radio's acting up again The battery cables must be loose I don't see any high tension wires around I like that though It says it so clear that the reason we believe is not that we want to get into a religious or scientific argument but that we want to be saved Now I was saved back there on that hill I know that for a fact I lost the burden that was killing my back and God turned me into something new and now I'm on my way to Life City The reason I know this. . . .

"Ladies and gentlemen, please excuse us once again for the unfavorable conditions in the atmosphere that are rendering our electronic presentation of this lecture difficult. We are making an all-out effort to correct the situation. We were about to say that scientific progress in New Testament studies has now moved into the field of linguistics. Some of the ablest scholars of today are now pointing out that such words as 'God,' 'Heaven' and 'salvation' no longer connote any meaning for humanity.

"This is not because of a change in the nature of the universe; indeed, we demons would have to insist that nothing in the universe has changed significantly since the disaster of nearly two thousand years ago. What has changed is modern man's focus of interest. He no longer troubles himself with speculation about religious matters. The very word 'spiritual' is dropping out of his vocabulary. Man has quite properly made himself and his environment the primary field of his study. To illustrate: in his psychosocial approach to behavior man has discovered that the primitive taboos on certain foods and the ancient Mosaic and Pauline injunctions on relations between the sexes are no longer needed. Possibly these strictures may have served some useful purpose in the childhood of the race (although that point is debatable), but today man has come of age and is no longer required to observe them.

"In fact, man's whole sense of values is undergoing a transformation, so that what he used to call bad he now calls good. He accepts what he finds in the world as 'given,' and looks upon 'sin'

as an outdated concept that is no longer significant. He is determined to make the most of every moment, to realize his full humanity, to exercise his potentialities to the utmost. He believes
that when he dies, he dies; that is all. Modern man looks with pity
on those shriveled souls who, under the impulse of some religious
illusion, continue to deny themselves the very things man was put
on earth to enjoy. In fact, he is inclined to look upon the whole
religious superstructure as a device to suppress man's free instincts
and to oppress his living conditions.

"Why shouldn't a man take what is offered to him? Why
shouldn't he enjoy the world? Why shouldn't he fill his life with
excitement and pleasure? Try to think of one good reason. There
is no reason. There is only the bogey-man, the 'social code,' or
as Dr. Freud liked to call it, the 'superego,' to which thinking
men and women no longer pay the least attention. Progress has
been extremely rapid in this area in recent years and we look for
greater things to come. . . ."

*Well yes that's the way I used to think back in Doomsdale
and it still makes some sense I mean you're a long time dead
like he says When I was on the road I know I couldn't see
why I should stay all night in a motel room when I could
go out and live it up You can't get away from the fact that
God wouldn't have made things pleasant if he hadn't expected us to enjoy them and I must admit I'm confused I
wish he'd shut up so I could have some time to think Ernie
old boy what do I do now Oh sure the next verse What else
OK "If any one is in Christ he is a new creation the old has
passed away behold the new has come" What Nothing about
fleeing fornication Ernie you're slipping This doesn't really
seem to apply the way I'm feeling right now Let's see "If
any one is in Christ he is a new creation the old has passed
away behold the new has come" Good night will you look*

at the sparks coming out of that radio If it's not the aerial there must be a short in the ignition somewhere You don't suppose these little verses are having any effect on the station program Why how could they It doesn't make sense but let's face it nothing else on this trip makes sense Let's try another and see "You who were dead in trespasses and the uncircumcision of your flesh God made alive together with him having forgiven us all our trespasses having canceled the bond which stood against us with its legal demands this he set aside nailing it to the cross He disarmed the principalities and powers and made a public example of them triumphing over them in him" Hey there's a fire in the radio Now what do I do I don't dare stop here Maybe I can pour some of this lemonade over it Wow that worked fast Well I sure got that baby's number I don't think he'll give me much trouble from now on Ernie old boy you did it again. . . .

"Ladies and gentlemen, we are very sorry indeed to report that some thoughtless transient driving through our territory has been firing unidentified flying objects into the atmosphere with such damaging regularity that we are unable to continue with this aaaawwwwwwkkk! rrrrrrrrrrrppppp! We had intended to continue the discussion by taking up the question of the end of theism, the sociological basis of the new morality, and the yyyyoooooowwwwwwkkkk! and political future of the modern church in a secular society. Instead we will be back tomorrow when we trust our magnetic field will be cleared and conditions will become more stabilized. This is Station WARP signing off and saying pppeeeeeyyyyoooppp. . . ."

So at last that man has decided to shut up What a relief He was a real snake oil merchant Had me swallowing everything I sure wouldn't stand up under a Communist brainwashing

Don't have the judgment or the stamina They'd have me
bleating Ho Ho Ho Chi Minh after about twelve seconds of
staring at the wall Yessir I Betrayed the People's Republic
I Dropped Germs in Your Water Supply *All right quit calling*
yourself names you can do better than that Seems like I ought
to be getting near the end of this miserable stretch What did
he call it Principality of Beelzebul Been climbing steadily
for half an hour now I can't make out if those are mountains
ahead Boy there must have been something loaded in those
Bible verses Can't figure it out Must have been God working
yet how could it through the car radio Oh well it's not my
war All this invisible tilting gives me the creeps anyway I'm
sure not worth it In fact the more I think about it I wonder
what it has to do with me and what I'm doing here Let's just
think again about that hill behind the transmitter Was I
saved there How do I know I was saved Could be I was just
talked into it I'm not denying anything just raising questions
When you look at my background all that might be as phony
as a three-dollar bill I haven't had any religious connections
Never went to church after tenth grade I'm proud I'm dis-
honest I lust after the flesh I have a colorful vocabulary that
is the admiration of all my friends I'm a spiritual deadhead
and a moral failure and to pretend anything else is to turn
me into a hypocrite which is worse yet I have no business
palming myself off as a good man I'm a blotch on the face of
humanity and ought to be flushed down the nearest drain
You open up my record all of it and there's not a church
board in the country that would vote me into membership
Godly matters are simply out of my reach I'm untrained and
ill-at-ease among people connected with religion Keeping up a
façade is hopeless I'm not adequate to the effort of faith

Simple reason is I'll never be any different from the person I know I am Even the thought of God these last few seconds fills me with loathing I'm a spiritual pervert incapable of holding a decent thought Those things I listened to on the radio were absolutely right There Is No God There Is No Son of God *The Bible is as full of holes as Swiss cheese I'm going to live it up I'm going to shout curses until this Principality is bleary with profanity and obscenity and holy smoke the car's heating up I'm losing power How can I get that radiator to cool down I don't dare stop in this hellhole There's something under my heel No wonder I can't work the throttle right That packet of verses It must have fallen off the dashboard Now they're spilled all over What's this one "Valley of the" something Nope I still can't get any power Oh man we're stopping right on the level only a few more yards and we could be going downhill Don't stall Don't stall Where's that gadget "Though I walk through the valley of the shadow of death I will fear no evil for thou art with me" Shucks that's where you are now This is the Valley of the Shadow of Death It was painted on the rock back there Once more "Though I walk through the valley of the shadow of death I will fear no evil for thou art with me" Huh I believe we're going to make it Just a bit more A bit more We're coasting I believe we're I believe we're we're we're Hallelujah we made it Ernie we made it God God God God I'm delivered The fear is gone That accuser is gone Those weren't my thoughts at all they were his After I jammed his radio program he started right in on my mind Well he can have those ideas straight back and may the good Lord rebuke him I'm over the invisible line Hallelujah. . . .*

Chapter 10

THE new stretch of road, while not paved, was an improvement over the route through Prone Valley, and it was evident that the topography was changing. The land was no longer desolate. Flocks of sheep and herds of cattle appeared here and there. An occasional barn and farmhouse could be made out in the distance. Chris let the Mustang roll down the winding slope until its engine cooled and began to function more normally. Water became an immediate necessity, and he was vastly relieved to find a small settlement, complete with filling station, coming into view. He turned over his vehicle to the mercies of a straw-haired young attendant, decided against discussing the adventure he had just come through, and went in search of food. He found none. A three-minute survey of the village's business establishments drew a blank; he was forced to return and open communications with the youth at the gas pump.

"Any eating places around here?"

"Nope."

"What do you call this—ah—"

"Airport City."

"Not really?"

"Really."

"Then where's the airport and where's the city?"

"Yer in the city. This road'll take you right past the airport. Ja know yer oil's down?"

"How's the water?"

"I ain't checked."

"Check out everything. And wash it."

An hour later his car was gleaming, ready to roll; and since Chris had ascertained from his gas merchant that a restaurant existed at the airport, he lost no time covering the few miles between. Approaching the site, he was disconcerted to find it unlike any airport he had ever patronized. A weird hush enveloped the scene. No planes were taking off or landing; dandelions bloomed in the landing strips; huge hangars stood bare with doors gaping; letters were missing from the road signs; taxicabs, limousines and car rentals were nonexistent; only a few badly weathered cars were in the parking lot. Porters were absent from the terminal entrance, where a sign read (of all things) NO LUGGAGE ALLOWED.

Chris parked the car and pushed through a door that had once been automatic. He found himself in a dimly lit waiting room with a few people sitting in it. Obviously the place had not had janitorial service in some time. Newspapers were strewn about; cobwebs festooned the telephone stalls. How long the people in the waiting room had been there he could only guess, but they seemed very much at home.

A buzz at one end of the lobby drew his attention. It was coming from the coffee shop, and he proceeded toward it. As he entered he found the restaurant offering a vivid contrast to the rest of the complex. It was crowded with people, some waiting, some eating, some sipping coffee, some holding intense discussions over open Bibles. Chris became aware that all eyes looked up at him. He paused, embarrassed, while a man perhaps five years his senior emerged from a booth and came toward him with hand outstretched.

"Chris Anders! God in your heart!" he cried. "It's me, Rusty Ness. From Doomsdale!" Chris took the hand and muttered, "Rusty?" He vaguely recalled a man by that name who had sold computers for a rival firm some years before. But that face! He definitely had seen that face recently. The stranger produced a card from his pocket, and Chris examined it.

LIFE CITY TOURS

T. (Rusty) Ness   *Consultant*

"You mean you left Doomsdale?" Chris asked tentatively.

"Man," boomed the other, "I left two months before you did. Have you eaten?"

"No. I—I'd like to."

"Sit down. I'm about to order."

The coffee shop resumed its conversational tone, and soon Chris and his friend were devouring steaks and sharing their harrowing experiences in a series of constant mutual interruptions. Ness had also been dismayed by his personal life and by the turn of world events; and having just come through a long siege of terminal cancer with his wife, he too had walked out the door and (with some help from Ernie van Gelst) had headed for the transmitter.

"That's where I saw you!" exclaimed Chris.

"Where?"

"It was a slide. The Major showed it. I remember his saying you had become a guide or something."

Ness smiled and continued his narration. He had run into a totally different set of circumstances from Chris, apparently, and had managed to get through to Life City, where he spent some time in a training program and was now making his first road trip on volunteer assignment. His eyes danced as he talked about it. "My job will be to organize tours to Life City. Can you imagine anything more exciting?"

"Well," deadpanned Chris, "I *can* think of a little excitement you might run into. Are you really going to shuttle people over this road from Poopout Hill?"

"Chris," said Ness, more quietly, "the road is not the same for everybody. I can't explain it, but it's true. I have a lot to learn. Probably I won't be stepping into the assignment in depth for at least a year, but that's the goal."

"So what do you do meanwhile?"

Ness made a face. "I've been assigned here," he said.

"Here!"

"That's right. For the next three months I'm the airport liaison officer."

Chris snorted. "This is no airport," he said. "There's no traffic, nothing. What are all these people doing here?"

"They're not doing anything. They're waiting."

"For what?" Chris asked.

A waitress came and filled their coffee cups. Ness lowered

his voice. "They think they're going to Life City direct by air," he said.

"From here?"

"From here!"

Chris took a covert look at the tables and booths, and whistled under his breath. The discussions had now reached a pitch of intensity; here and there voices were being raised.

"So what do you plan to tell 'em?" he asked.

Ness took a long swallow before answering. "I'll just talk to them. Try to share with them what I've learned."

"Such as?"

"It's important to hit the road."

Chris shook his head. "That road is a headache," he said. "If I thought there was an airlift to Life City I'd wait right here with them."

"Exactly," said Ness, leaning over and speaking very low. "I'd be waiting with you. Of course it could take place any time, but meanwhile look at what's happening. They're perched around here like pigeons. This place is getting run-down and the people ingrown. Do you think the Lord will honor that? It seems as if all these people can think about is, 'Will there be a seat saved for me?' "

"No flight schedules are posted," Chris observed.

"That's the point. Nobody knows when the airport will become operational. But meanwhile all over the world the devil and his Principalities are working overtime, and there are millions of people, I can tell you, who have never even heard there is a Life City."

"Tell me about the city," said Chris, mentally switching channels. "What is it really like?"

"My pleasure," said Ness. "It's the most intriguing, the most enticing, the most challenging place you ever saw. I can hardly wait to get back."

"I've heard all that," said Chris. "Try to be specific."

"All right." Ness took out a pencil and began scratching on a paper napkin. "Life City is divided into two parts. Ever been to Budapest? Or Kansas City? It's kind of like that. Two cities with a broad river between, only it's the same city. Now, this side of Life City is the only part I've visited. It's the same side those other people have come from that you've met—van Gelst, the four sisters, the transmitter staff, and so on. They operate out of this side. But the airport is across the river, you see, and once you get over there, your volunteer service on this side is all done. I mean, it's finished. Now these people"—he waggled his pencil at the crowd in the restaurant—"want to fly direct to the Life City airport. I've been given the job of trying to convince them that they should go by road and check in on this side, so they can join the rest of us on volunteer assignments until it's time to be picked up and taken across the river."

Chris shook his head. "Good luck," he said. His further reflections were cancelled out by a thin, dignified gentleman with white hair and a shiny serge suit who stopped by their table. "I happened to see you come in," he said, clearing his throat and smiling a hollow sort of smile, "and I just thought I'd leave you gentlemen something to read." Pulling a wrinkled tract from his pocket, he dropped it ostentatiously on the table. It was printed in small type on newsprint under the bold heading, PREPARE TO MEET THY GOD.

"That's very nice of you," said Chris, waiting for him to depart; but the man was not so disposed.

"I've been up yonder on the observation deck all day watching," he said, "and I just asked the Lord to send me somebody to warn. Always looking for little ways to serve him, making the moments count."

"My name's Ness," said Rusty, holding out his hand, "and this is Mr. Anders. We're glad to meet you, brother."

"I tell you," said the older man, "we're living in perilous times. I do believe—"

"That reminds me," interrupted Chris, "did Red China fire its bomb?"

"Not yet," murmured Ness. "Soviet Russia just got into the act." He turned to the visitor. "Excuse us, brother—what did you say your name was?"

"I didn't say," was the reply. "It's Quacious. L. O. Quacious. Now if I may just sit down here a moment, brethren, I would like to discuss one of the more important issues of life with you." Ness moved over and Mr. Quacious seated himself with a sigh. "I do like profitable conversation," he said. "There are so many promises and consolations in the Word, and so many false opinions about, that I find it a signal ministry just to talk to people and help them understand the need for faith and watchfulness, and for a work of grace in the soul."

"What was the issue you wanted to talk about?" inquired Ness.

"Anything you like. Things on earth or things in Heaven; things past or things to come; things moral or things spiritual —just so it be profitable, mind you. Would you ask the waitress to bring some coffee?"

"You know," said Chris, leaning back in his seat, "I'd like to hear about that business of a work of grace in the soul."

Ness nodded. "All right, sir," he said. "How does the saving grace of God reveal itself when it is in the heart of a man?"

"Now there is an intelligent question," said Quacious, brushing the dandruff from his sleeve. "I have written an excursus on the subject which I hope to publish some day. Let me say first of all, and briefly, that where the grace of God is in the heart, it causes a great outcry against sin. Then second—"

"Hold on," spoke up Ness. "I'm not sure I buy that."

"Why not?" inquired Chris.

"Because I think it is more accurate to say that the grace of God shows itself by inclining a man to give up his own sin— to abhor it, in fact."

"But what difference is there," protested Quacious, "between crying out against sin and abhorring it?"

"Look," said Ness, warming up, "it's the easiest thing in the world to sound off about sin. I can work up a head of steam about the way some character is acting and keep right on serving the devil in my heart. I seem to remember that Potiphar's wife had a great deal to say about sin; she said she had been raped, but she lied in her teeth. What's your second point?"

Quacious' chin trembled slightly as he began again. "Why, I—I would say God was working in a man's heart if the man showed a great knowledge of Bible teaching."

Ness shook his head. "I won't buy that either," he said earnestly. "A man can have all the Bible knowledge in the world without being a child of God. You can know every proof text, every commentary, every spiritual secret, every sign of prophecy, and still be lost and on your way to hell."

Quacious sat bolt upright and smacked his lips. "This is certainly not an edifying conversation," he said.

"Rusty," put in Chris, "you're working our friend over for his views, but you're not saying what you yourself think. Maybe you'd better tell us now about the signs of God's grace working in a man's heart."

"Was I rude?" asked Ness. "I'm sorry. But I could wish someone had been a little ruder to me when I was mixed up all those years. I wish someone had taken time to show me the plan of salvation. Let me give you what I learned in Life City. When the Spirit of God convicts a man's heart, that's a sure indication that grace is at work. The man comes to understand that he is dead wrong in the eyes of God; that unless he finds mercy through faith in Jesus Christ, he is really on his way to eternal separation from his Lord. Then the grace of God is at work when a man makes a commitment, when he dedicates his life to Jesus Christ, and confesses his sin, and receives Christ as his Savior and Lord. Finally, the grace of God is shown when a man exhibits a holy life in his daily behavior and shows love to his fellow man by reaching out to human need, while subjecting himself to the authority of God's Word."

"Now, I like that," said Chris. "I sure hope I can get into a class like that when I get there."

"I must say," said Mr. Quacious, rising to his feet and speaking in a quavering voice, "I find it very unsettling. Some of the new ideas being bandied about today are not my idea of the simple old Gospel. We have been warned about great swelling words and clouds without water. But I shall carry on." He picked the tract off the table and stuffed it into his pocket.

"Wait a moment, Mr. Quacious," said Ness, trying to change his tone. "Aren't you getting tired of sitting on that observation deck? Wouldn't you like me to schedule you on a bus tour I'm working up that will be leaving soon for Life City? We could surely use your knowledge and background in some of the classes there."

"I shall wait here," said the old man, rolling his eyes. "Watch and wait. Be sure you're not the ones left behind. Beware! Prepare!" And he was gone.

There was a pause at the table. "At least he could have thanked you for the coffee," Chris commented.

Ness smiled a rueful smile. "You have now been phased in to my current assignment," he said.

"Ring-a-ding-ding," said Chris.

"Oh, it's all right. I'll talk to him some more."

"Look," said Chris, "this place is giving me the creeps. How about phasing out of it long enough to run a special tour?"

"For you?"

"Why not? There's the Mustang standing out there, all gassed up. Just roll me right on into Life City—that's your job, isn't it?"

Ness took a miniature walkie-talkie from his jacket pocket and began a conversation with some distant communication center. In a few moments he was receiving instructions. He looked up. "I can do it," he told Chris, "but it won't be easy."

"That makes it par for the course," said Chris.

"Beware!" grinned Ness.

"Charge!" said Chris.

Chapter 11

"YOU might be pleased to know," said Ness as they drove away from the airport, "that we're through with the desert. From now on it's thickly settled."

"That's very nice," returned Chris, checking his mileage. "What I really want to know is which road we're taking."

"Just follow the signs leading to the Fair."

"What fair?"

"The World's Fair. What else?"

"So we're going to a fair now, are we?" Chris shook his head. "This is funny. First I'm told what a sinner I am, and naturally it's true. So I get saved, and I'm given a route map and put on the turnpike to Life City. And where does it take me? Down the gayway!"

"That's right."

"Why not take a bypass? There should be plenty of them."

"Because that's the way it is. If you want to get to Life City, you have to go through the World's Fair."

"Where is this carnival?"

"In the middle of Pridesburg. That's the capital. It's about three hours' drive to the checkpoint."

"Capital!" Chris was struck by a chilling thought. "Do you mean we're going to have to run through another of those Principality things?"

"This one usually doesn't give us any trouble."

They drove on in silence for an hour.

It was just ten years ago that we took that trip to the gulf with Tom and Sally Man Eileen looked pretty and did we have fun I wonder if Christians ever have fun like that old Quacious didn't look as if he'd had a good time since his fifth birthday Do you suppose Jesus had fun I bet he did Well if they blow up the world it's all over anyway I guess the only answer is get to Life City as fast as I can but I don't dig this Fair jazz. . . .

The road took on the appearance of an expressway leading to a large metropolitan area. Signs began to appear saying VISIT ABADDONLAND, THE WORLD'S FAIR. Traffic increased. After some time Chris commented, "Hear that? I think it's a wheel bearing."

"I didn't know what it was," said Rusty, "but I've been thinking we'd better start looking for a place to spend the night. We'll be coming to the checkpoint in another sixty miles or so. The only place I know is the Borderline Motel just outside the city, and they're full. I called them from the airport."

"Can't we find a place in Pridesburg?"

"It's not advisable. You're in enemy territory. How long can we go on that bearing?"

"I dunno."

"Well, maybe we can get a night's sleep along here some-place."

But when they did spot a motel, it invariably had a NO VACANCY sign hung out. Some special event in town had crowded the accommodations all along the route, and with darkness coming on they held council. They could return to the airport (where the lone hostel was overflowing with air-lift-watchers), or go on back to Airport City (which had no hotels or motels at all), or try sleeping by the roadside. Neither of them was inclined to backtrack, so they finally pulled into a rest area and tried to doze in the car. It proved a cramping experience, especially for Chris, who was still feeling the effects of combat. The evening being warm and pleasant, the two travelers eventually lifted out the rear seat of the Mustang and set it on a grassy spot. Spreading an auto robe and their topcoats, they settled themselves for rest. Rusty asked to have the car lights left on while he turned in his Bible to the eighth chapter of Matthew.

"Want to hear it?" he asked.

"Be my guest," said Chris, yawning.

" 'Now when Jesus saw great crowds around him, he gave orders to go over to the other side. And a scribe came up and said to him, "Teacher, I will follow you wherever you go." And Jesus said to him, "Foxes have holes, and birds of the air have nests; but the Son of man has nowhere to lay his head." ' That's funny, I had a feeling there was something Biblical about this arrangement. Seems our Lord did it."

Chris reached under his hip and removed a stone. "I don't want a hole and I don't want a nest," he grunted. "I'll just settle for a sheet of foam rubber."

Despite the dew, despite the morning crispness, despite the ground which failed to become softer as the night wore on, despite a certain stiffness of neck, they awoke refreshed. After washing their faces at the rest area drinking faucet and offering a brief prayer, they set off in the car down the turnpike looking for food (the girls' lunchbasket had long since been exhausted). Their search carried them clear to the Borderline Motel, which indeed proved hospitable. They were given opportunity to shave and make themselves presentable, and were then filled with ham and eggs, toast, and coffee.

"You know what," said Chris after draining his third cup, "with prayer and coffee I don't care what's up ahead!"

"I never had any flak going through Pridesburg," said Rusty, "but you can't tell. Maybe this is their day off. That could explain the cars on the road. It would mean that people were moving around, going to church and to the Fair and all."

"Church! In a Principality of the devil?"

"Oh, there are lots of churches here. These people are quite religious—didn't you know? They believe the Bible."

"But what kind of churches?"

"Well, this is Abaddon's Principality, so of course there's a First Church of Abaddon. Then there are people here from other Principalities, so we have the First Church of Belial—"

"I'll skip that church," said Chris.

"—and the First Church of Beelzebul, and the First Church of Apollyon."

"Which one outranks the others?"

"There's a big cathedral down town known as the Mother Church, the Temple of Satan. It's an old building and the services are supposed to be quite formal."

"But what do they do in these places? Curse and spit and hold Black Masses?"

"Only on special occasions, so I've been told. When the worshipers get sluggish and indifferent they try to stir them up, but usually the services are milder. They give slide lectures about primitive magic, or reports on the latest anthropological cave discoveries. They hold Wednesday evening sneer meetings when they come to hear testimonies by people who have fallen from grace. It's hard to get such people to talk, I've heard. They have to pay good money to get them. But on Wednesdays they also tell stories ridiculing Christian believers. Then on Sunday nights they schedule historic films that describe how religious leaders of the past tortured and persecuted people who differed with them. At special seasons they honor the heroes of their church—Judas, Nero, Tamerlane, Attila, Hitler, Stalin and all that crowd."

"I can't believe it. Who do they pray to?"

"To the demons, of course."

"Demons!"

"Yes, but be careful. In Pridesburg they say that the demons are really good spirits, the disembodied principles of human enlightenment."

"I know that's a lie."

"Naturally. But they're building a tremendous tower to one of the chief demons at the World's Fair. You can see it once we get inside the gate. It's called the Temple of Lucifer. They say it just keeps on going up and up. I suppose you know Lucifer was an angel of light before he fell from Heaven."

"I'm not up on my demonology," said Chris, "but it looks as if I will be. Just so he doesn't get into my wheel bearing."

As they paid their check they learned from the cashier that all garages in the vicinity were closed, so there was no chance of a repair job. They drove on another mile and traffic began to slow down. Chris could see barbed-wire barricades in the distance. Directly ahead was the checkpoint with a series of booths manned by uniformed and heavily armed troopers. One of them stepped out to look over the Mustang.

"May I see your entry permits?" he asked.

Ness leaned over. "Officer," he said, "we have our passports and we're going on to Life City."

Immediately the trooper's expression changed. "Not to-day," he said. "The city's closed to through traffic."

"But why?"

"It's an unholiday in Pridesburg. They're celebrating the nineteen-hundredth anniversary of the fall of Jerusalem. You'll have to pull around and turn back."

"Officer," said Chris, "I've seen you before somewhere."

"Could be. Your plates were issued in my home town."

"Doomsdale?"

"Right."

"Look, sir," Ness tried again, "it's early; couldn't we just go right on through? We don't have any plans to stop and we'll keep our windows rolled up."

The trooper's face was a mask. "Pull over," he said. He guided them into a parking lot where they waited for him. When he arrived he was carrying an attaché case. "Just coming off duty," he explained. "I'm Sergeant Manly Hooper," and he extended his hand.

Both travelers were startled by this unexpected turn, but Ness recovered first. "I'm going to take a long chance, Sergeant," he said. "Have you ever been to the transmitter?"

The trooper frowned. "Let me warn you to watch what you say," he said. "There's a linguistics center on the sixtieth floor of the Temple of Lucifer, and they have what they call a Babel wave that can pick up audio signals all over town."

"I can take care of that," said Ness. He took out his walkie-talkie and pressed a switch. It responded with a tiny, high-pitched squeal. "Go on with what you were saying, Sergeant," he urged.

The trooper walked around to the other side of the car. "Let me in," he said. Then he continued, "It was a long shot, Mr. Ness, but you were right. Would you like to hear about it?"

"We sure would."

"I set out for Life City with my family two years ago. We didn't like some of the things we saw happening around us. We got along pretty well until we came to Pridesburg, but I ran into some trouble here. I got away from the Lord and began living a secret life. After that it seemed foolish to take any more risks, so I decided to lie low. I reported to Infernal Affairs, and discovered that anyone from Doomsdale was welcome to stay as long as he wanted. The only problem was, they kept my passport."

"Your Bible?" asked Chris.

"Yes. They put me on this traffic job, and after a year I was promoted to sergeant. Meanwhile my family began to fall apart at the seams." His eyes became suspiciously moist.

"Well, now, Sergeant, what are our real chances of making it through?" asked Ness.

"You'd better not try it today."

"Why not?"

"There's an ugly mood abroad. Three teen-agers slipped

through the barbed wire last week to try to make it to Life City. Now they've slapped on a curfew."

"But they have to let us through," protested Ness. "They're required to honor our passports."

"Not on unholidays. There are huge crowds moving into the Fair, and the police won't guarantee your safety."

"Sergeant," said Chris quietly, "why don't you ride along with us? They won't stop us if they see you. Then we'll all get through."

Hooper shook his head. "Spiritually I'm ready to come, but I've got my family to think about," he said.

"Even so. I've got a wife and four boys back in Doomsdale. Is your family ready to go?"

The Sergeant gave a frustrated laugh. "They used to say they were, but the two girls have got me worried. They went to church last week, and my wife told me one of them was offered two hundred dollars to testify at one of their sneer meetings. I think Mary Anne would like to leave, all right, but not without them."

"You're in the same boat I am," said Chris. "If they won't leave, you can't make 'em."

Hooper peered out the window. "If I thought God wanted me to go with you and then try to come back for them, I'd say let's go."

"Do you have a car?" asked Ness.

"Yes, and I'm being watched. Tell you what: you wait here, and when you see my Valiant moving onto the expressway, you follow me. Here are two entry permits in case you get stopped, and here are two passes for the Fair." He got out of the car and leaned on the window. "Thank you for stopping by, gentlemen," he said. "Do you see this gun?" and he patted his revolver. "I know I haven't been true to the Lord, but if my daughter had gone through with her plan, I was going to blow my brains out. I guess that's why he sent you."

"Does that mean you're coming with us?"

"It does."

"God in your heart, Sergeant," said Rusty.

As the Mustang was already past the checkpoint, it was easy for Chris to pick up the Sergeant's Valiant and follow it. They swung into the main stream of traffic and saw looming ahead of them the Temple of Lucifer, an astonishing ziggurat of a building that dominated the landscape. Hooper turned down a side street and they followed a mile or so until he drew up in front of a residence.

"I'm leaving my car here at the house," he explained. "They can use it."

"Try to get them to come with us," said Ness.

"Can't. They're all at the Fair." He went into the house and emerged in twenty minutes, dressed in civilian clothes and carrying a suitcase. The Mustang then headed back to the thoroughfare and they drove on until it became a parkway, and a huge gate appeared with the sign, WELCOME TO ABADDONLAND, THE WORLD'S FAIR. The road continued through the gate, where Hooper saw them past the guards. Then they drove into the fairgrounds, following bumper-to-bumper traffic, keeping their doors locked and their windows rolled up.

At first appearance the Fair seemed to Chris to follow a rather conventional "expo" pattern. Cultural and scientific exhibits from the various Principalities were housed in buildings that impressed him as outlandish and bizarre; the cumulative modern effect, he decided, was depressing. Here and there some distinctive features were to be noted. A jagged pile of concrete on one corner celebrated MAN THE ANIMAL, while a white rounded structure surmounted by a cupola advertised itself as the HOUSE OF BAAL, THE ORIGINAL CULT OF FERTILITY. Next to it was a concession ride called the TUNNEL OF PERVERSION. A waiting crowd had gathered around an aluminum-and-glass building labeled INSTITUTE OF PORNO-GRAPHIC RESEARCH. A few doors farther they drove alongside a broad plaza in front of the Temple of Lucifer. Chris slowed down and gaped in astonishment at this great pile and the imposing series of fifty-foot-high sculptures that led to its entrance.

"When I was here before," Rusty commented, "I was told that these statues form a group called THE PRIDE OF LIFE, which is designed to glorify the human race, human ambition and human achievement. It seems they represent man as tri-umphant over his religious and superstitious past and master of his destiny in time and space. If you look, you can see one figure stepping on the broken tables of the Jewish law and another crunching a cross in his fist. Two others are break-ing down the spires of a cathedral." Chris stared at the wild ensemble of bulging biceps, clenched fists, jutting jaws, and arrogant expressions, and sank back in his seat rubbing his eyes.

"If man is all that great," he reflected, "he ought to be farther along than he is. What bothers me is that I can't figure out who's behind this Fair. Is it man's show or is it the devil's?"

"Good question," nodded Rusty. At that moment they passed a trailer parked by the curb, and a bright light suddenly flashed down on them from the roof of an adjacent exhibit building. A girl wearing a bikini slipped out of the crowds on the sidewalk and, to the astonishment of Chris and Rusty, jumped up and sat on the hood of the Mustang. At the same time police whistles sounded, television cameras rolled up from nowhere, flash bulbs began to pop, and four young men in red pantaloons and matador capes surrounded the little car.

"God help us," groaned Rusty, "it's a disaster. Get something going!"

Chris felt the button under his open shirt collar. "All-prayer," he said.

Now the young men were tapping on the glass and insisting that the windows be rolled down. "Welcome to Pridesburg and Abaddonland!" said one of them, smiling. "Out of the tens of thousands of visitors to our World's Fair today, you have been chosen by our computer to become Special Guests of the Unholiday. A marvelous program has been planned for you. Congratulations!" A patter of applause went up from the curious who were gathering on the sidewalk.

Manly Hooper, who had been in the back seat talking into his two-way radio, now punched Chris on the shoulder. "I'll take your car and meet you with it outside the city gate," he said.

"Which gate?" asked Chris, panicking.

"The Pridesburg east gate. It's a big spiked barrier set in an arch. Outside there's a freeway all the way to Life City."

"But—we're caught. We can't even get out of this Fair—"

"There's an exit straight ahead," yelled Hooper in the increasing hubbub. "Look for—" But before he could finish the sentence Chris was lifted bodily out of the car by two matadors and carried past the cheering crowd to a waiting white Diabolo 98. There he was joined by Rusty in the open tonneau, then by the girl in the bikini, who sat between them and waved to the crowd as they moved slowly ahead. When the big car passed the Mustang, they spotted Hooper behind the wheel showing his badge to the police.

The Diabolo proceeded down the boulevard a mile or so and stopped before a reviewing stand which overlooked a grassy military parade ground in the center of the Fair. Chris and Rusty were taken by the matadors to the stand and presented to various Fair functionaries. They were then seated and exposed to an interminable program of gymnastics, equestrian jumping, chorus competitions and a reading of prize poems on the theme, "God is dead." An eager young man with a transistor tape recorder finally joined them, obviously for purposes of an interview.

"You are from our sister city in Doomsdale, are you not, Mr. Anders?" he asked.

"That's right."

"Your occupation?"

"Computer salesman."

"We are very happy to have you visiting us. How long do you expect to stay?"

"Not sure."

"What do you think of Pridesburg, Mr. Ness?"

"We have met only one of your citizens," said Ness, "but we think he is a most outstanding person."

When the briefing was over, Rusty took Chris aside.

"Anders, old boy," he said, "it's not going to work. But praise the Lord anyhow."

"What do you mean?" Chris suddenly felt weak.

Ness took out his New Testament and covered it with a program. "Listen to this: 'You shall even be brought before governors and kings for My sake, as a testimony to them.' We're not going to double-talk our way out of this one."

"But they'll kill us! You heard what Hooper said. Once they find out the score, the ball game's over."

"So?" A smile played about Rusty's lips.

I really believe this man's not afraid to die But boy I sure am I mean I'm ready to meet the Lord but to face this mob is something else Why did we have to fall into this Ever since I left that transmitter it's just been trouble and more trouble I thought it was supposed to be love joy peace and freedom I feel like a chicken about to have its neck wrung Where's that button. . . .

Chapter **12**

THE eager young reporter now returned and escorted Chris and Rusty from the reviewing stand to a comfortable reception room in an adjoining clubhouse. There he introduced them to a man who was waiting to greet them with a cigarette holder in the corner of his mouth. He proved to be Mr. Max Spirochete of the Abaddonland public relations staff.

"Well, gentlemen, you have been turned into celebrities by the fickle goddess of chance," he said with a grin. "I hope you enjoyed the show this afternoon, and I hope even more that you enjoy what we have planned for you."

"That all depends," began Rusty. "We'd like to—"

"Two young ladies, selected by a popularity poll, have been provided as your escorts," went on Spirochete, unheeding. "You will be meeting them in the studio next door. After our formal interview with the press and TV you will be officially presented from the reviewing stand to the great unholiday crowd. A chauffeur will then drive you and your girl friends to a private dining spot on the edge of the city. And then"—Spirochete's face became a smirk—"an evening of pleasure awaits you at a place we call the *Court and Sport.* But first, gentlemen, business. I must familiarize myself more with your background since you are to be my guests. We'll start with you, Mr. Anders."

"If you don't mind," interrupted Rusty, "I would like to be taken first."

"Of course. You are Mr. Ness, are you not? Tell me what parts of the Fair have appealed to you."

"We really haven't seen it, you know. We were just passing through when they stopped us."

"Ah, yes. And you are coming from—"

"I'm from Doomsdale originally."

"We both are," said Chris.

"Well, you will want to visit our Doomsdale Pavilion tomorrow. It's considered socially quite significant. You'll find it right behind the Garden of Sodom. You did say you were a tour guide, didn't you, Mr. Ness?"

"That's right."

"Then you should be bringing some chartered groups here to see these exhibits. Are you operating out of Doomsdale?"

"Well, I hope to be." Chris had taken off his all-prayer button and had slipped it into Rusty's hand. Rusty now looked at it, and his shoulders squared the slightest bit. "My headquarters are in Life City," he said. "We're heading there now."

Spirochete carefully put down the cigarette holder. "You are Christians?" he asked. They nodded. Spirochete closed

his notebook and stood up with a glassy look in his eyes.)
"You will wait here for instructions," he said, and left the
room.

Rusty looked at Chris. "Let's pray," he said. For the next
twenty minutes they moved into another dimension of existence, so much so that they hardly noticed when an armed
guard stepped in and quietly took a position by the door.
At last Spirochete returned, his face still impassive.

"If I may interrupt, gentlemen," he said, "it is forbidden
to offer prayers in this Principality to anyone or anything
but evil spirits, on penalty of death." He put a fresh cigarette
in his holder. "Your plans for this evening have been revised.
It seems your arrival has come at an opportune time and will
prove of great advantage to our kingdom of darkness. This
will deprive you of some pleasant company this evening,
which is unfortunate. But our people have been showing
signs of slackness. There has been a drop-off in religious
interest. I must confess that I too am guilty—I have not been
to a Black Mass in over a year. My superiors have informed
me that attendance at religious services this morning was
computed at five percentage points below a year ago."

"We sold you that computer," said Chris. "I remember the
shipping order."

"How interesting. And now you will help us again, for we
are going to recognize you with a special Act of Apostasy
tonight."

"Where?" asked Ness.

"Right here at the parade ground. They are announcing
it now from the studio."

"If you don't mind, Mr. Spirochete," said Rusty, standing

up, "we have other plans. Our passports are valid and in
order, and you are expected to honor them. We want to go
on through the city. We appreciate the favor you have shown
us, but our business is more important than yours."

"A debatable point," said Spirochete, smiling. "Let me
examine your passports."

"They are in the car. Coming here was not our idea, you
will remember."

"It does not matter; you will not be needing the passports.
Please sit down. You are to remain in this room; some food is
being brought in."

"Why are you keeping us?" demanded Rusty. "We have
committed no offense against your city. We had tickets and
passes."

"You forget that you entered it illegally on an unholiday.
I trust you like deviled ham. . . ?"

By seven o'clock the entrances to the parade ground were
jammed with unholidaymakers seeking admission. The word
had circulated quickly, for Acts of Apostasy were popular in
Pridesburg. As the crowd swelled in numbers a murmur of
subdued excitement filled the air punctuated by occasional
catcalls. Many of the new arrivals carried signs placarding
four-letter words and oaths that reflected the spirit of the
evening. Lively dance music blared out from a combo that
announced itself (on its bass drum) as the *Damnation Army
Swingers*. As Chris and Rusty were marched out to the reviewing stand by a detail of bayoneted soldiers, a great roar
went up from those massed in the center of the parade
ground. Shouting and gesticulating was carried on until a
tall, grim, white-haired man in a military tunic came to the

podium and held up his hands for silence. The band gave a fanfare. Spirochete now stepped to a side microphone and said, "Men and women of Pridesburg, guests of Abaddonland, we bid you welcome and present to you our distinguished master of ceremonies, his excellency, the Commander-in-chief of the armies of Magog, Marshal of the Legion, General Pitt!"

Amid cheers the white-haired figure then spoke: "On the occasion of this great Act of Apostasy I bring you greetings from your profane lord, his Ultimate Bottomness, the Archimandrite of the Abyss, the Father of Lies, our own Depth of Being!" The responding roar became deafening, then broke down into a kind of chant.

"What are they saying?" whispered Chris, his voice trembling.

"They're yelling, 'Take off their clothes,'" replied Rusty. "They don't like the cut of the outfits they gave us on the hill. Seems it's the wrong style in Pridesburg."

"What'll we do?"

"Trust God. This crowd is high on booze and dope. Look over by the entrances, you can see the bottles being passed out."

"Aren't you afraid?" asked Chris.

"Was Stephen afraid?" retorted Rusty.

"Who?"

"Stephen the Apostle."

"I don't know if he was or not. Why do you ask?"

"Just came over me," said Rusty. "Somehow I felt very close to him."

The General had quieted the chanters and was now intoning, "It is the Great Accuser's desire to recall the people of this Principality to their natural goals of indifference, self-interest and self-indulgence."

"Nice choice of words," murmured Chris. "The old boy can sure push his product."

"His stuff is all cranked out and screened by the linguistics center," whispered Rusty. "Every public utterance is controlled."

"Tonight," the General was saying, "we are celebrating the nineteen-hundredth anniversary of the fall of Jerusalem with a special televised pageant. Among other spectacular numbers, the Brimstone Company players will present from this platform a brilliant reproduction of the desecration of the temple" (here he was interrupted by another series of shouts). "And for your enjoyment, we are adding as the climax a very special Act of Apostasy" (the howling became more shrill).

"These people want blood," said Rusty grimly. He handed the all-prayer button back to Chris.

"Let me, at the beginning of the evening," said the General, "present to you the men who are the principals in our Act. They were arrested this morning within the walls of our Principality, right on the fairgrounds, through the brilliant counterespionage work of our intelligence agents. At the time," the General turned to look scornfully upon Chris and Rusty, "they were illegally and deceitfully attempting to sneak through the heart of our glorious Abaddonland and to escape into enemy territory. They claimed to have passports, but they have been unable to produce them to the authorities. We sought in our innocence to do them honor, only to discover by clever interrogation that they are people most unwelcome in our midst."

Ugly, flushed faces crowded to the front of the reviewing

stand, and Chris noted that bottles were being brandished threateningly. "Get out of the way, General," a voice shouted. "Let us at 'em!"

But the General held up his arms. "I sympathize completely with you," he called out, "but I must ask you to restrain yourselves. We have a long-standing tradition in Pridesburg that everyone is accepted within our Principality on his own free responsibility. It is true that we do not like spies, but these men have a right to establish their own guilt and corruption. I present them now to state their position, and ask you to remain silent while they speak."

He motioned to Chris and Rusty, and immediately Rusty walked forward and seized the microphone. "Citizens of Pridesburg and friends," he said in an emotionally stirred voice, "I bring you greetings in the name of the Lord Jesus Christ, the King of Heaven. He has commissioned my brother Chris and me to share with you the good news of God's free salvation in Christ Jesus. I call upon you tonight in our risen Savior's name to renounce Satan and all his works, to repent, and seek the face of the Lord. From the bottom of my heart I plead with you to receive the gift of life that Jesus Christ offers to you now in love, and which he made possible through his death on the cross for your sins." The crowd began to growl, and Rusty pitched his voice higher. "Brethren!" he cried. "The forces of evil you serve are doomed to destruction. Come back! Come back to God! He is the only true God. He loves you! He will save you!"

By the time Rusty reached the word "save" the howling had reached a crescendo that drowned out all further speech. Up to this point Chris had sat transfixed by Rusty's display of courage; now he looked around to discover that the reviewing stand was completely empty. General Pitt, Spirochete, the guards and the band had all quietly disappeared. A bottle crashed against the podium and shivered. As he ducked, Chris saw Rusty attempting to crawl behind it. He himself dropped on all fours and barricaded himself behind a chair. Bottles were now smashing everywhere as the crowd shrieked and roared. Chris heard Rusty cry out. Then a bottle struck his own ankle and broke. He felt the blood oozing inside his sock.

Suddenly the lights on the reviewing stand went out, and shadowy, yelling figures began to clamber on the platform. A voice whispered fiercely to Chris, "Come with me!" It was a girl carrying a large, heavy poster which she now used to shield them from the flying bottles. Together they slid off the stand to the ground, where she dropped the sign and dove through the bunting underneath the platform. Chris followed her. As they groped through the undershoring they could hear frenzied people overhead stamping and crying, "Kick him! Kill him! Lynch him! Cut his throat! Where'd the other one go?"

"God in your heart, Rusty," Chris muttered as he limped after his guide to the back of the stand and through a hole that had been freshly cut in the wire fence surrounding the parade ground. Once through the hole they were met by a young man who stepped out of the shadows and whispered, "This way!" By now the lights were turned on again and they could hear military officers barking orders. The young man led them to some bushes outside a building, where two Hondas were concealed.

"Get on behind David," said the girl, "and don't speak."

The two little vehicles sped through the nearly empty fairgrounds as the shouts of the crowd gradually became fainter. The young man, David, now turned his head. "Can you hear me?"

"Yes."

"We've got two gates to pass. One is the exit from the Fair, the other is the iron gate of the city. The Babel wave has been picking up our movements from the tower, so we can expect UFO's to start coming our way."

As he spoke a bright streak shot through the sky overhead, then another. "There they are," said David. Chris patted the all-prayer button in his pocket and remembered something.

"God!" he shouted. "Neutralize!"

"What's that mean?" asked David.

"I haven't the slightest idea," said Chris. "All I know is, it works."

By the time they approached the east Fair exit, the UFO storm had begun to subside, and the Hondas held a rendezvous behind a concession booth. It was discovered that only two patrolmen were manning the gate that was open for vehicular traffic.

"The trouble is," said David, "the tower has alerted them and they're watching for us. It looks as if they haven't had time to set up a real roadblock, but if we try to run for it they'll simply mow us down."

"Listen!" whispered the girl. A roaring noise was approaching, and it turned out to be the sound of a giant helicopter, approaching from the east and flying at an extremely low altitude. The copter swooped down over the main control booth to the Fair gate and caused both guards, who appeared with drawn guns, to throw themselves on the floor. Immediately David lurched ahead in his Honda and raced through the exit, followed by the girl. They pursued a devious course across the city in the direction from which the helicopter had come. After five miles of zigzagging and dodging down side streets, David stopped again. In the distance they could hear the sound of police sirens.

"We are a quarter of a mile from the iron gate," he said. "We'll wait here for the helicopter to come back."

"How do you know it's coming back?" asked Chris.

"You should ask us!" said the girl. "You've got the all-prayer button."

"Must be the Lord," said David.

"But where is the copter?" asked Chris.

The girl put her hand on his arm. "They went to get your friend," she said gently. "They're taking him across the river."

"Who are?"

"The three men you met on the hill."

"The ones with the grease on them?"

"They're the ones. They're now a rescue crew. They've just about landed on the parade ground by this time."

"But with all that drunken mob—"

"The people are used to it. They just scatter and clear a space. Nobody ever opens fire on that helicopter."

"Then why didn't we wait and get picked up too?"

David smiled and hesitated. "You want to go with them?"

"I want to be with Rusty."

"You'd better wait. Here they come. They're going to make another pass, and we've got to get through that iron gate or else."

"Dad should be outside with your Mustang," added the girl as she started her Honda.

"Your dad—" began Chris.

"Here we go!" called out David. The giant helicopter was bearing down on the huge old gate, its engines wide open, its twin blades whirring. It came within three feet of the entry booths and the waiting guards flattened themselves. Immediately the two Hondas emerged from behind an outbuilding. As they came to the archway there was a clanking sound and suddenly, mysteriously, one of the ancient iron portals creaked open on its hinges just enough to allow the vehicles to slip through. Shots rang out of the dark behind them. Chris, hugging his young driver, shouted, "Praise the Lord!" and looked up to see a greased arm waving to him from the cockpit of the helicopter. He could make out a vague form sitting next to the pilot. Chris waved back until his eyes filled and he could no longer see.

Chapter 13

A SHORT distance from the city gate David brought his Honda to a halt and pointed to a dark object lying in the middle of the freeway. It proved to be (as Chris had guessed) a pouch dropped from the helicopter. On opening it David took out a dispatch case and read by the light of his vehicle, "Proceed to Oasis Motel one mile ahead, where you will find Mustang. Your rooms have been reserved and your lodging paid for. Get a good rest, you deserve it. *l Mbit* God in your heart. [*signed*] The Hikers."

It was not long before a tearful reunion took place in the lobby of the motel between Manly Hooper and his daughter. After a few moments the Sergeant greeted David and then Chris. Hooper invited them to bow their heads in prayer while he thanked God for deliverance and asked him to rescue the remainder of his family from darkness. Then Hooper said to Chris, "Friend, I would like the honor of presenting my youngest, Doris. I never expected to see her

again. She and I have been separated by the generation gap—
that's just one of the gaps in Pridesburg. But something
occurred tonight at the Fair while she was listening to your
friend Rusty."

"What was that?" asked Chris.

"Let her speak for herself."

Doris looked at her father and then at Chris. "I found the
Lord," she said gravely.

Chris smiled as he took her hand and looked into the pretty,
freckled face mostly hidden by wild-appearing hair. "What
a wonderful thing to happen," he said. "I might have guessed
you were Hooper's daughter. You saved my life, and I only
wish it could have been Rusty's."

"I didn't do anything," she protested.

"Just tell me why you did it."

Doris wrinkled her nose. "I really expected us all to die,"
she said. "You know, ever since my sister went to that sneer
meeting a week ago I've been—well, kind of bothered. Then
when Mr. Ness talked to the people the way he did about
Christ, I knew what it was. God spoke to me right there."

"But you must have known something before," said Chris.
"You had the escape all worked out."

"That's because we heard a rumor that Dad had been
arrested with you. But I didn't see him anywhere. Then
when they started the Act of Apostasy, and I saw that your
friend was the main target and had already been hit, I
decided to try to get you out."

"Did you kill the stage lights?" asked Chris.

"I don't know. I just saw a cord as I was climbing up the
front, and pulled it."

"What a girl!"

"Mr. Anders," said Doris, "you had a lot more going for you than that. I don't understand how the UFO's suddenly stopped, and the copter showed up, and the guards disappeared, and the iron gate opened by itself, and all the rest. It was like a movie."

"A very remarkable person named Charity gave me a button," said Chris, reaching in his pocket. "It says all-prayer. That's the answer."

Hooper laid his hand on the broad-shouldered young man next to him. "David," he said, "you risked your life in this business without even knowing why."

"Say it was the excitement," David grinned.

"Or the gal?" Chris raised an eyebrow.

David continued: "I did catch some of what Mr. Ness was saying to the people before they drowned him out. I could hear him on the amplifier but I'm not sure I followed his meaning. Anyway, that package we picked up back there should help."

"What was in it?"

David lifted his arms. "Three passports to Life City: one for Doris, one for her papa and one for me."

"Praise the Lord!" said Manly. "We live again! A new copy of God's Word. And may I say that this is one Bible that won't get lost in Pridesburg, or Doomsdale, or Sodom or Gomorrah."

They retired soon afterward, and the next day was spent quietly at the motel putting their clothes in order and attending to various ailments. Doris had received a number of minor cuts from broken glass. Chris spent a long time soaking his ankle. In the afternoon they all gathered at the swimming pool and shared a study hour together with their Bibles.

Here it was decided they would continue on to Life City with the three vehicles until they received further instructions. Hooper reported that the Mustang's wheel bearing had been repaired, that road conditions were excellent and good weather was promised. Accordingly after another night's sleep, breakfast and prayer, the little caravan checked out of the Oasis Motel and took to the freeway. The Mustang assumed the lead with Chris driving, and the two Hondas followed. Hooper—a sergeant no more—had outfitted himself in slacks and a wool shirt for the trip.

"I believe," said Chris, as the Mustang purred through a grassy upland, "that a sheep is about as stupid an animal as you'll find on this earth."

"Not necessarily," rejoined Hooper. "Sheep can be trained. Besides, they don't make war, or choke the atmosphere, or kill the fish."

"No, but look at 'em nibbling out there, ruining the pasture. Sheep seem to operate purely by herd instinct. Never go where they're supposed to. Utterly helpless to defend themselves. I say they have no brains whatever, just solid mutton."

"Perhaps," mused Hooper, "that's why our Lord called us sheep."

"I'd resent that," grinned Chris, "if it were from someone else. Now you take a computer—there's something that makes sense."

"You're not serious," said Hooper, "but I can tell you they are very serious about computers in Pridesburg. In fact they are making plans to canonize one next year some time. They say it's the first step toward making it an idol."

Chris' eyes glistened. "Think of the advertising program you could work up to kick it off. 'Process Control proudly announces its first Demon!' " The Mustang began to swerve and he pulled it back. "Perhaps I'd better blow that subject. Do you realize we're climbing again?"

"I believe we're in the Delectable Mountains," said Hooper. "The summit is about six thousand feet."

"Rusty used to talk about these hills," reflected Chris. "If that's where we are, we're in fruit country. And there's some kind of—I forget what he called it, but it was a—"

"Camp meeting?"

"Probably."

With the two Hondas following, they wound into a fertile valley where the grassland was interrupted by small orchards and farms abounding in a variety of fruit- and nut-bearing trees. Roadside stands offered samplings of fresh delicacies. After a stop or two they reached the summit in late morning and began a descent into open range country. By noon they had arrived at a roadside sign: GOSPEL CAMP MEETING AND BAR-BECUE, ALL HANDS INVITED.

"That's what I call timing," said Chris, looking at his watch as he pulled up to wait for the Hondas. "David," he called out as the young man drew alongside, "how do you like your steak?"

"Right now, sir," was the rejoinder.

Less than a quarter-mile off the road they found the encampment in a cuplike valley surrounded by hills on which cattle were grazing. Cars, trailers and cabins were grouped about a clump of trees at a sort of spa or watering place. The focal point of activity was a large, rectangular structure consisting of a corrugated tin roof set on poles. Underneath it a barbecue pit gave off succulent smells of roasting meat and strong coffee. Scores of persons in casual country dress were lined up in front of the pavilion, and as the four travelers made a hesitant approach they were welcomed and loaded down with paper plates, napkins, knives, forks and coffee mugs.

An easygoing atmosphere prevailed. At the end of the shed a cowboy with guitar was twanging,

> All my sins are gone,
> All because of Calvary. . . .

During lunch it developed that Bible study was over for the day and the afternoon was to be given to rest and recreation. Since the new arrivals were still feeling the effects of their escape from Abaddonland and hospitality was eagerly pressed upon them, they elected to remain overnight. After some rearrangment, a double and a single cabin were made available, and that evening the travelers joined several hundred others in a warm evangelistic service held under a full moon, with a tree stump serving as pulpit and Coleman lamps providing illumination. The leathery-faced speaker was introduced as the Reverend André LaBourd, a local sheepherder. His message was from John 10:11, "The good shepherd giveth his life for the sheep." It was a beautiful discourse, filled with homely illustrations of pastoral life. At one point he asked his audience to lean back and fix its gaze on the stars.

"We who herd sheep in the Delectable Mountains hear things at night that others sleep through," he said. "We hear the cry of a sick lamb. We sometimes hear a coyote pack disturbing the flock. But we also hear music. The Bible teaches that the stars make glorious music. Listen with your heart and you will hear them now, singing, 'Glory to God in the highest, and on earth peace.' That is because someone is coming home to God tonight. Someone is going to put his life in the hands of his Creator, and say, 'Come into my heart, Lord Jesus.' *Voila!* That is why the stars sing. That is what the shepherd hears. And you can hear it too."

When the invitation was given David and Doris were among those who rose to their feet and walked forward to commit their lives to Jesus Christ. A score of other campers joined them in front of the oak stump, and they were given instruction in Bible study by some young volunteers. The shepherd-pastor then invited Chris and Manly to his trailer, where they sat outside in camp chairs and enjoyed a glass of iced tea.

"I must say I was deeply moved by what you said tonight," confessed Chris. "Could I inquire about your accent?"

LaBourd's face broke into a hundred wrinkles as he smiled. "I'm a Basque," he said. "All sheepherders are Basques. The shepherds at Bethlehem were Basques. You did not know this?"

Chris parried the question. "So you have been to Life City and are back here on special assignment," he said.

"But of course. It is better to be with Christ, but until that time I stay here. And we see people coming every night to Christ."

"Then what happens to them?"

"Tomorrow you will learn. Now I would like to hear a special report from you, Monsieur Anders. You see, last report I got on your voyage was from Pilgrims' Manor House. I believe you spent the night there."

"You mean, Pastor, that you've been following this crazy junket of mine?"

"Monsieur, there have been more eyes following you than you imagine."

Chris filled his glass with fresh tea. "Why is it that the trials of a Christian are so much more difficult than an unbeliever's?" he asked.

LaBourd smiled. "Perhaps you will now illustrate. Then we shall interpret."

"Well," said Chris, "coming down from the Manor House I felt really good, I remember. Then when I got to Prone Valley I met this Belial. Do you know him?"

"Every Christian is acquainted with Belial," said the shepherd. "I suppose he called you fake."

"He certainly did."

"Ah, yes. Unfortunately it is so. By ourselves we are all fakes and pretenses. That is why we must depend utterly upon Christ to live the Christian life. Prone Valley is where we are humiliated before the Lord."

"So that's it. I thought it was called Prone Valley because Belial was knocking everybody on his good behavior with that wrench of his."

The Basque waited for him to continue.

"Well, of course I had the all-prayer button that one of the girls had given me, and I remembered that stamp on my forehead, but what really got me past Belial, I think, was the aerial. It lit up like a Christmas tree. I figured that meant something or other, so I broke it off, and whenever Belial tried to finish me off I touched him with it."

"What was this weapon, Monsieur?"

"The aerial on my little car."

"Ah. And what did it do to this Belial?"

"It kind of stunned him and made him scratch as if something was chafing him."

"Of course. Evil always tries to overreach, my brother; then the good Lord steps in and binds the strong man with invisible restraints."

"But what was the aerial, Pastor? I think I know, but it never was clearly explained to me."

"In the sixth chapter of Ephesians the Apostle tells us about the armor of the Lord. The last piece we are told to put on is the sword of the Spirit, which is the Word of God."

"I know what the Word of God is, all right. It's a book. But—"

"*Non,* Monsieur. It is more than a book. It is a weapon to be grasped and used against the evil obstacles of life."

"Well, praise God, it worked."

"How did you get past this Belial?"

"I left him squirming under his bulldozer in a ditch full of dead men's bones."

"Let me say to you something, Monsieur Anders. If you ever voyage back over that road, he will be waiting for you, no?"

Chris paused a moment before responding. "I'm aware of that, Pastor," he said, "because two fellows did turn back, and I know what happened to them. I may not savvy much about the Christian life, but I'm staying out of that man's way."

"So then?"

"So then I came to the next Principality—whose was it— Beelzebul's? I think so. And here they tried to brainwash me right through the car radio. Pumped a lot of theological language at me that sounded real smooth, but I was using some of Ernie van Gelst's Bible verses, and when I'd repeat one it would jam their broadcast."

"Ah yes. This was the magnetic field, I think. But did you answer their arguments? That is important too."

"How could I? They were talking about linguistics and taboos and myths and the superego and I don't know what-all. It was a good pitch, and at first I bought the package, though I wasn't too happy about it coming from demons."

"Monsieur, it is no package. What they say is *raisonnable*, and you must answer it with *raison*. A verse will protect your soul for a time but will not fully satisfy your mind. There are answers—Bible answers—to all these things. You must find them. It is a lifelong study. This was all?"

"No. Then the worst began. They didn't use their radio beam, they had some other way of planting twisted thoughts directly into my mind. I ended up wanting to curse and scream and kill people. Then I found that verse about 'Though I walk through the valley of the shadow of death, I will fear no evil: for thou art with me.' That finally brought me through."

LaBourd nodded his lean head. "A young disciple cannot be entrusted to his own judgment when evil powers really attack. Only the Word of the Lord will save him. So?"

"So I drove on to the airport and met my friend." Chris began to feel tired. "I guess I won't talk about him. The others can tell you the rest of the story."

"Mr. Ness was a fine man," said LaBourd. "He stayed here once."

Do you suppose this old-timer might have the answer Rusty must have been hit by a thousand whiskey bottles but if

he was dead why did they bother to come for the body I'm
supposed to know all these things out of the Bible but I
don't seem to know anything Anybody who tries to program
a curve of Christian growth on me is wasting his time. . . .

Chris put an imploring note in his voice. "Pastor," he
said, "I know I'm dumb, but was Rusty dead or wasn't he?"

"*Mon ami,*" said the Basque, "the corpse, it is nothing. To
resuscitate it, what is that? You rub the heart; it dies again.
But to pass over from death to life, *cela,* that is for all who
are in Christ Jesus. Your friend left here still alive after the
flesh; he arrives on the other side a new creation with a body
magnifique. Yes? We do not question God's time. The vision
has its own appointed hour. *A Christ 'la gloire.*"

"OK. So when we cross the river, that's the moment of
truth."

"*Oui,* Monsieur."

"Then just one more question. How could this helicopter
crew go flitting back and forth taking people to glory without using retro-rockets or something like that to bring them
back into human existence?"

"Ah, that is another tale, and its secret is locked up in
the stars. These men are on detached angel service. The clue
lies in the grease on their bodies."

"Where do they get that grease?"

"Not from this solar system. You see, it not only protects
from the fiery darts of the wicked, but from the last enemy
himself. Even so, it is quite an assignation to fly the river.
They are brave men, those *montagnards.*"

Chapter 14

CHRIS sat up in bed and looked at the blanketed form across the room. Manly Hooper lay inert. Rising, Chris walked to the window, favoring a rather stiff ankle. He squinted at the sunshine of a clear mountain morning and saw campers in bright jackets already lining up under the tin roof for their bacon and eggs and hotcakes. Something in the distance caught his eye: a familiar black Chevelle parked by a cabin. Sure enough, there was Ernie van Gelst walking toward the mess hall, chatting with Doris and David. Pulling on a pair of pants and a jacket and jamming his feet into his shoes, Chris ran a hand through his hair and stepped outside.

"Ernie!" he called.

Van Gelst came toward him, the young people following.

"How are you getting on, Anders?" he asked, shaking hands.

"Still operating, though I don't quite know how. Welcome to the Delectable Mountains."

"Yes. And congratulations to you on getting through Pridesburg."

"We lost a wonderful man there," said Chris, the timbre of his voice changing.

"Let's get the priorities straight," replied van Gelst evenly. "That was no loss, it was pure gain. A revival has broken out at the Fair since you left as a result of Ness' testimony."

"It's very exciting," said Doris. "We heard it over the radio. I just pray that my mother and sister were reached."

"What do you mean, revival?" asked Chris.

"Why, people have been going to church and interrupting the Black Mass by singing Gospel choruses they've learned over Station WEAL. They've been standing outside the Temple of Lucifer, shouting 'Praise the Lord!' and passing out New Testaments and inviting people to receive Christ. It was so serious that martial law had to be declared."

"I miss Rusty," said Chris simply.

"You're going to miss some other friends, too." Van Gelst turned to the young people. "You folks can take off after prayer if you like. I'll be dropping in on you farther along. Got plenty of fuel?"

"These don't take much," said David, patting his Honda with a grin.

"Where are you sending them?" Chris wanted to know.

"To the transmitter," said van Gelst briefly.

"Without any breakfast?"

"We're all fed and filled and ready to go, sir," reported David, testing the lashing of his gear.

"I've been there once," explained Doris, "but I'm going back with Dave."

By now Doris' father had emerged from the cabin and there

was a half-hour of prayers and farewells all around. As the Hondas buzzed off, van Gelst left to see some other converts of the night before, and Chris and Manly retired to the cabin to shave. Later on as they were enjoying their coffee under the tin roof, their friend rejoined them and they began raising questions about the route that lay before them.

"It's all good road," van Gelst assured them, "but you will still have problems. Basically it's the same thing you have had to contend with all along the line. It's the problem that tied up Hooper in Pridesburg for two years."

"What's that?" asked Manly.

"Your heart. Yourself." A New Testament came out of the breast pocket. "I'm going to give you a verse to help you. It's in Romans, ninth chapter, sixteenth verse: 'So then it is not of him that willeth, nor of him that runneth, but of God that sheweth mercy.' "

"Now you've given it to us," Chris, "tell us what it means."

"It means you can't make it on your own." Van Gelst rose. "Sorry, gentlemen, I just spotted another candidate for the transmitter." He reached in his pocket for two verse cards and handed one to Chris and the other to Manly. "Use these when you go through the gate at Life City. God in your heart!"

Within a short while the Mustang was back on the freeway with Hooper at the wheel and Chris sitting alongside, munching a pear and studying the cross-references in his Bible. They came to an interchange just as Chris looked up.

"What did the sign say?" he asked.

"I noticed it just as we passed," Manly replied. "Guess I was thinking about Mary Anne. I believe it said DETOUR.

meaning to bear right, but I'm not sure. Shall I go back and look?"

"OK, but we can't turn around here," said Chris. "Keep right and we'll go on to the next overpass." The freeway continued to unroll before them, and Chris went back for the moment to his studying. "Willeth . . . runneth . . . shoo-eth mercy," he muttered. "I hope I can figure out something about that before we run into trouble."

"Think fast," said Hooper, swinging over to the shoulder. "We're in trouble now."

A siren uttered a low growl behind them as Chris turned around to discover bright red lights flashing at him. His heart leaped to his larynx. "What did we do?" he wondered.

"Nothing," said Manly. "Don't move. Make him come to us."

A husky, uniformed officer got out of the patrol car and walked over. "May I see your license, please?" he asked Hooper. He examined the document and handed it back. "Pridesburg police, eh? I'll ask you to follow me into the township. We turn off at the next interchange."

"You've written no ticket," Manly pointed out. "There has been no traffic violation."

"This is the township of DeSpare," said the officer sternly. "All roads here are private roads. You are trespassing. Follow me."

They trailed the police car to the interchange and then to a small settlement where they drew up before a one-story civic building marked TOWN HALL. Here they were ushered into a courtroom where a uniformed bailiff bade them be seated. The policeman took up guard duty at the door. After a few minutes an old man entered the room through a door at the front. He carried a large, thick book and a gavel, and used the latter to pound the table three times. Chris and Manly and the bailiff stood up.

"This honorable court of the township of DeSpare," intoned the clerk, "is now in session. Justice Korah T. Failing, presiding."

At this point the front door opened again, and a small, youngish black-haired man with a shoebrush mustache entered the room. He wore his justice robes loosely, and upon assuming his seat at the bench he began lighting a pipe. "What's the charge?" he asked.

"Usual," replied the clerk, reading a note the patrolman had handed him. "Driving through the township of DeSpare without authorization."

Judge Failing smiled what seemed to Chris a villainous smile. "Anywhere else, gentlemen," he said, "this would be a trivial matter, but the township of DeSpare operates under its own unique legal code. Grave crimes here are lightly considered, while small infractions receive heavy penalties." He puffed a while. "You could draw a life sentence for this offense. How do you plead?"

"Not guilty," Chris and Manly both answered.

"It doesn't matter. We are going to hold you without bail for a while, not to investigate but to assist in your mental conditioning. Next week we'll see how you are coming. Court is adjourned."

The jail turned out to be a cell block in the basement. The bailiff escorted them down and delivered them to a massive, dull-looking young man who informed them that there would be no food or water till next day, so there was no point in asking for it. The heavy door at the foot of the stairs clanged shut, and they were left to grope in the near-blackness. Eventually they found two cots slung from the wall, and sat down for a conference.

"Well, here we are, Paul and Silas," said Manly.

"But just five hours ago I was feeling so good," complained Chris. "I was full of hotcakes and coffee, and thought everything was going the way the Lord wanted it."

At ten o'clock next morning the dull young man opened the door to the cell block. "My orders are," he said, "not to feed you but to beat you up." There followed a frightful half-hour in which the huge jailer, armed with a rubber hose, belted both men into senselessness despite their valiant efforts to defend themselves. The fact that visibility was so poor made the nightmare even worse. At last the jailer withdrew, leaving them broken and prostrate on the floor, and locked the door behind him.

On Monday morning, two days later, the prisoners were brought upstairs to the courtroom. Having received no nourishment since their incarceration, both men felt faint and weak. They were also blinded by the light in the room. After Judge Failing entered and court was convened, chairs were provided and they were permitted to sit down. The magistrate puffed his pipe and studied them, the same smile on his face.

"How are you coming in your thinking?" he asked.

"Sir," whispered Hooper, "whatever the offense was that we committed, we believe we have served our sentence. We would ask to be released."

Judge Failing shook his head. "You don't get the message,"

he said. "This is not really a jail, it is a school. You are going through a learning experience. What I'm interested in is, have you been absorbing it?"

"We have had no food or water," said Chris hoarsely. "We have been horribly beaten, but no one has looked after our injuries. We have been subjected to treatment far worse than animals. Is that what you're trying to teach us?"

"Precisely," said the smiling judge. "If you are as comfortable as possible I will now discuss your case with you. We are quite aware, you see, that you two are pilgrims on your way to Life City. You thought in fact that you had just about arrived. Now if we seem to be using relatively harsh measures during your sojourn in DeSpare, let me assure you our basic purpose is altruistic. We wish to make clear that you are not angels, but animals—or let us say, natural creatures. You are, as the Bible says, born of the flesh, and the gulf between spirit and flesh is so vast that none of us will ever cross it.

"You have entertained high hopes of getting to Heaven, gentlemen, but they are earthly hopes. They were fabricated out of the molecular action of your brains. You imagined that you could tool your little yellow car right through the gates of St. Peter, with children strewing flowers in your path. Now the aim of this court is to bring you back to reality by demonstrating that the flesh is totally inadequate to make it into the Kingdom of God; that it has always been so and always will be. Even while you turn your mind to thoughts about the Kingdom, you see, your real nature is lusting for satisfaction and enjoyment. We do not consider this bad, nor is it good; it is simply a fact of life.

"Let's take the defendant Anders here as an illustration.

I know, sir, that you are rather confused by the things that have been happening to you on this journey. You are like a rudderless derelict on the high seas. You don't know what's going on or where you stand. If I were to ask you point-blank, 'Are you a Christian?' you would probably answer, 'I think so,' or, 'I hope so.' Wouldn't you, now?"

"I—" began Chris.

"Of course you would. But if I were to ask you, 'Do you drink water through your mouth?' (assuming we give you some water), or if I should ask you, 'Do you hear through your ears?' there would be no hesitation in your answer. That is because you are by nature not spiritual at all, but biological. Millions upon millions of years ago your ancestors were crawling through the primeval slime along the equator, looking for unicellular life to feed upon. And that, essentially, is all you are. Now tell me, Mr. Anders, how can an organism that has emerged out of such an environment—a blob, if you please—aspire to a spiritual level of existence? It simply doesn't make sense. If I may quote the Bible, the leopard cannot change its spots.

"It's easy to pretend you are a spiritual type, Mr. Anders, and I believe you have been doing a lot of pretending on this journey. You have taken on the protective coloration of those around you. That, too, is a biological behavior pattern. But now the string has run out; you have landed in the township of DeSpare, and it is our job to establish the triumph of the flesh—"

"We are nothing like what you say," interrupted Manly Hooper. "We are children of God."

"Silence in the court!" roared the bailiff.

Judge Failing shrugged his shoulders. "Who isn't? You

are a part of the natural order. Dogs, elephants, mosquitoes, the fish in the sea, all are children of God. When you forget this you are in trouble, as you are now. Why is it that one of man's oldest yearnings is to want to be immortal? He invents his gods and his messiahs and his heavenly palaces because he cannot endure to be locked into the prison of his flesh. He thinks he is terribly important, therefore he decides to be a child of God, so he can live forever. But I am here to teach you the truth of the matter. Do you know what the secret of life is?" He got up from his bench and walked around to where the prisioners were seated.

"Hold out your hand," he said quietly to Chris.

Chris looked dubiously at Manly, whereupon the bailiff bellowed at him, "Hold out yer hand like his honor said!" Chris obliged; and the judge promptly knocked the hot ashes from his pipe into the prisoner's open palm. Chris gasped and pulled back, shaking his hand.

"You see," said the judge, going back to his bench and taking out his tobacco pouch, "that is the real answer. The secret of life is death. We all die, for we are all mortal. Now the question is, how do we get the mastery over death? By letting it creep up on us and choke us with a wasting disease, or by going forth boldly to meet it?" He reached into a drawer of his bench and took out two small vials. "I want you gentlemen to face the issue squarely. You are not going to make it to Life City because you do not have the qualifications or credentials. As your apostle put it, 'They that are in the flesh cannot please God.' We have made you painfully aware that you are in your bodies, and you are not about to climb out of them into some ectoplasmic existence.

"You can try, and try, and try to make it into Life City;

you can think all the holy thoughts you want; you can memorize your Bible and spend every waking moment praying; you can be baptized the whole length of the Jordan River, but it will do no good. You simply do not have what it takes. Tell me, gentlemen, what could God do with you in Life City, with all your selfish, lustful and vindictive ideas? With all your pride and vanity? You would be the blind trying to lead the blind.

"But," Judge Failing smiled again, "we are going to give you a way out. Inside each of these vials is a small needle. We are going to send you back to your cell and invite you, some time between now and tomorrow morning, to break the seal and to prick your skin. That's all you need to do; just prick yourself anywhere with that needle. In twenty seconds it will be all over. In that way you will make yourself a conqueror of the natural order. You will achieve your mastery over life. Believe me, gentlemen, it is the only way for you."

The bailiff stepped over, picked up the vials and held them out to Chris and Manly. "Take them," he said menacingly. They did.

"Now before court is adjourned," said the justice, "let me add one more warning. Your young friend Mr. Doubts, who worked you over the other day, will be back down to see you bright and early tomorrow. If I were you I'd give him the slip before then. You now have the means to do so." He rose and left the room, and the prisoners were returned to their cell block, where they fell into an exhausted sleep.

"Well," said Chris several hours later, as they sat in the darkness, "it looks as if he's right. The string has run out. I don't think I can take another beating."

"Before I forget it," said Manly, "give me your vial."

"Why?"

"Because the Bible says, 'Thou shalt not kill,' and that means we're not to take our own lives either."

Chris slowly handed over the vial, and Manly smashed them both against the wall of the cell.

"Got your all-prayer button?" asked Manly.

"Nope," said Chris. "I must have lost it in that fight. You know"—he cleared his throat—"if we don't get some water by tomorrow, I won't be able to talk."

"I've been thinking about that verse," said Manly.

"What verse?"

"Ernie's verse. 'Not of him that willeth, nor of him that runneth, but of God that sheweth mercy.' "

"Have you figured out what it means?"

"Well, it kept coming to me while that bird was lecturing us in court. It says the same thing he was saying, in a way. We can't make it on our own strength. If we get there, it will be by the grace of God. I think Paul was talking about the cross —something done for us that we couldn't do for ourselves."

"So all our good intentions end in disaster. Like when the transmission goes out in the Mustang."

"Or the universal joint," nodded Manly.

"But it doesn't matter, because it's God who brings us to himself. He provides the transportation. That it?"

"That's it," said Manly.

Chris stood up and began to pace back and forth in the cell. "This whole thing is ridiculous, being in here," he said.

"How do you mean?"

"I mean we had no business on earth letting ourselves get

drawn into a deal like this. What's the name of this judge? Failing! What's the name of this place? DeSpare! What's the name of this jailer? Doubts! You and I are not working for these clowns. We belong to the Lord! The only reason they've got us salted away is that we let ourselves be put here. Isn't that right?"

"I don't know about that," said Manly. "Last time I tried that cell door it was pretty solid metal."

"Think, man, think!" cried Chris. "We've got to use our skulls. Doesn't the New Testament say something about God making a way to escape?"

"Yes, but I've forgotten the verse."

"All right, let's go over some of the Psalms. There's one, I think, that says, 'In all thy ways acknowledge him, and he shall direct thy paths.' "

"That's not the Psalms, that's Proverbs," said Manly. "But there is a Psalm that says, 'I shall not die, but live, and declare the works of the Lord.' "

"That's the idea. We're just not going to stay here, that's all. We're moving out. Keep coming, now. Let's have another."

" 'Teach me thy way, O Lord, and lead me in a plain path, because of mine enemies.' "

"What's that in?"

"The Twenty-seventh Psalm. It was always my favorite, even in Pridesburg. Listen to this: 'The Lord is my light and my salvation; whom shall I fear? The Lord is the strength of my life; of whom shall I be afraid?' "

"Man, that's all we need. Now look, you've got some keys in your pocket, haven't you?"

"Not for that lock."

"How do you know? Have you tried them?"

Manly rose slowly and went over to the door. "Try these, too," said Chris, holding out a set. "They took my car keys, but I always carry a spare."

The barred jail door was secured by a small lock that operated from the outside. By reaching through the grillwork, Hooper could insert a key, but in each case it failed even to penetrate the lock.

"I noticed this lock when we first came in," he said. "It's a Yale. Nothing else will work."

"Let's not quit," Chris insisted. "What other keys do you have?"

"None."

"All right, let's just double-check. Let's empty out everything we've got right here." The blackness was almost total, so that they could only feel what they placed on one of the cots, but they went about it thoroughly. "Take everything out of your wallet," said Chris.

"Why?"

"We're looking for a miracle, aren't we? How can we— wait! Here's something." Chris pulled out an identification card from his own wallet. "I think I remember them making up this plastic card at the transmitter. Major Putter gave it to me. Feel it. Doesn't it seem thick to you?"

Manly ran his fingers over it. "Could be something inside," he said.

Chris scraped the edge of the card against the wall until the plastic opened. Then with Hooper cupping his hands, Chris shook out a slim steel key. "This is the God who shows mercy," he said. "I just know it's a Yale."

The key fitted snugly into the lock, and the cell door

creaked ajar. Within thirty seconds the two prisoners had collected their things and were tiptoeing up the stairway. They found the building dark and empty, it being past midnight. The front door of the town hall was secured, but Major Putter's pass key fitted this lock too.

"Hold it!" whispered Chris. "Before you turn that lock, here's a drinking fountain!"

Given a new burst of life by the water, they pushed out the door, touching off a burglar alarm. They raced to the rear of the building, where they located the Mustang in a parking lot. Within minutes they were back on the interchange, heading out of the township as fast as rubber would take them.

"Do you see that patrol car?" asked Chris.

"I see some lights flashing back there," said Manly.

"Good-bye, DeSpare," murmured Chris, opening the throttle a bit more. "Give me another Psalm."

"How about this? 'The Lord preserveth the simple: I was brought low, and he helped me.' "

"Excellent. More!"

" 'I will walk before the Lord in the land of the living . . . for thou hast delivered my soul from death, mine eyes from tears, and my feet from falling.' "

"Did you say falling or failing?"

"Well, I guess you could say both!"

"Amen! See if there's anything to eat in the car."

Chapter 15

AS THEY descended the mountain range Chris reached out a hand, tapped Manly on the knee and pointed ahead. Amid some low wooded hills in the far distance, flashing in the rays of the early morning sun, stretched a skyline of magnificent proportions. White towers seemed to become almost incandescent as they lifted their turrets to a cloudless sky.

"Is that it?" asked Manly, almost unable to complete the question.

Chris nodded. "I'm dead sure of it. Nothing else like it on the whole route. Hang on, buddy, it means glory ahead."

"Makes you kind of shiver, doesn't it?" muttered Hooper.

"Can't exactly say it does," replied Chris. "I just feel good all over. It's as if this poor, unglued frame of mine was telling me, 'Now we're going to come together.' I just wonder if they serve manna for breakfast."

The freeway stretched like a twin ribbon across the green valley as the travelers sped quickly toward their destination. Dipping to the valley floor, they found lakes beginning to appear in pockets of the rolling hills. Local traffic was picking up; not infrequently a car passed them in the opposite direction, obviously geared for a long journey. An hour later they reached the attractive environs of the city. Before them loomed a series of tall, imposing aluminumlike pillars that formed a belt around the metropolitan area. They were at a loss to explain these striking columns, and Manly was still puzzling over them when Chris pulled off the road, drove into the parking lot of a handsome restaurant complex and stopped in front of a gas pump.

"What are you doing?" demanded Hooper.

"Do I have to explain?" retorted Chris. "Talk to your stomach."

His passenger continued to protest. "We're so close to the end of the trip, let's take it on in. It's just a mile or two."

Chris gave the attendant instructions for a thorough checkup and a wash job. "I'm not saying Life City can wait," he philosophized. "I'm just afraid I can't. The way the Lord put this carcass together, he never intended it to get so low on fuel. Remember how he fed the five thousand?"

"Well," murmured Hooper, "when you put it in language like that—"

The restaurant was crowded, but the hostess offered to seat them at a table where two other men were already waiting for their orders. Chris accepted the suggestion and they found themselves opposite the two strangers who soon introduced themselves. One said he was John Densely; the other, the Reverend Freddie Phemeral. The formalities out of the way, Chris ventured, "I take it this is Life City."

"Not quite," said the clergyman, "but almost. Been traveling long?"

"Yes and no," said Chris. "For the last few days we've

been a little out of touch." He felt the bruises on his cheek-bone but said no more.

"You haven't heard the news?" asked Densely.

"No."

"Well! This morning the Russians joined China's nuclear war threat. Said we had twenty-four hours to begin airlifting troops out of Berlin."

"It never ends, does it?" commented Hooper.

"What never ends?"

"Oh, things. Just one uproar after another."

"It keeps getting worse," said Phemeral. "Within hours it may all be over."

"Maybe and maybe not," said Manly. "The Lord might have something to do with that." He placed his order, then asked, "Are you gentlemen here on business?"

"In a way," said Densely. "We're Christians on our way into Life City."

"Great!" exclaimed Chris. "You've been through the transmitter too, have you?"

Densely looked at his companion. "You see," he said hesitantly, "we're not pilgrims in the ordinary sense. The doctor here is working on some sociological studies. He'll be engaging in research in Life City. Me, I'm going in as—as a kind of tourist."

"I thought—" began Chris, but Manly interrupted him.

"Tell me, Brother Densely," he said, "how are things between you and God?"

Densely lifted his nose slightly in the air. "About as well as they are with you, I expect. I think about God a lot."

"So does Belial," murmured Chris.

"What do you think?" persisted Manly.

"Oh, I'm not sure what you're looking for, Mr. Hooper. That's a rather impertinent question, you know. But if you're one of the orthodox types, let's say I reflect on occasion about Christ dying for all men, and about my own personal dedication to his service. That means a lot to me."

By this time the food had arrived for Densely and Phemeral and the conversation was diverted to more casual topics. The doctor was soon describing the studies in motivation which had led him to seek admission to Life City. "I'm very much interested in the individual ethical act, or as you might say, the good deed," he explained. "I want to investigate the philosophical background and equipment that make up a person's desire to do such a deed. Does the breakdown of contributing elements yield any significant rationale? Are there any guidelines here? Is it all sudden impulse or environmental pressure, or are there genetic factors? What part does culture play? What about the effect of sibling training? And so on."

"But what led you to try to do research in Life City?" asked Manly.

"Well, I happen to know that in Life City many people are being sent out on missions to help their fellow men. There's a strong sense of social responsibility here. I hope to do some spot interviews and perhaps distribute some questionnaire materials."

"Will you be using computers?" asked Chris from force of habit.

"Definitely. I've taken two courses in programing, myself. We'll be feeding the results into computers as fast as we collect them."

The rest of the meal passed amiably enough, and as they rose from the table together Chris asked whether Densely and Phemeral had transportation to the gates of the city. It so happened that they did; accordingly they parted, and Chris and Manly went to the service station to wait for the Mustang. Before long they were embarked on the final stage of their journey; but they were so interested in discussing the conversation in the restaurant, they scarcely noticed the breathtaking appearance of the main approach as they drove up to the city entrance, where the freeway ended. Chris broke off at last to call attention to the fascinating architectural sights surrounding them on all sides. "Look!" he cried. "We wondered what those aluminum pillars were. The whole city seems to be walled with some kind of insulated glass, and the pillars make the frames!"

A young attendant in white shirt and trousers now stopped them and offered to take the Mustang to a garage inside so they could proceed on foot through the arched portal. "Everybody enters this city on his two feet if he can walk," he explained with a smile.

"Don't we have to take off our shoes?" asked Chris, remembering a temple he had once visited.

"No sir," was the reply. "You'll be issued new sandals inside. But it's important that you carry your Bibles with you. They're your passports, you know."

They fished the Bibles from the glove compartment and climbed out of the car. Before they could start walking across the plaza to the portal, however, they were greeted by two men who turned out to be their erstwhile luncheon companions, Densely and Phemeral. "It's a relief to find you here," said Densely. "We've been having some difficulty gaining admission, and we need someone to vouch for us."

"Let's just sit down for a minute," said Hooper, indicating

a marble bench beside a fountain. "What did they say to you?"

"Why," said Densely, "it's rather ridiculous, but the man in the first booth asked whether we had Bibles. I see you've got yours. You know, I thought about bringing mine, but in the rush of leaving it slipped my mind. As I recall, it wasn't where I thought we kept it. But the doctor here has a whole briefcase full of religious documents of one kind or another, and they wouldn't let him through either. '

"I noticed at the restaurant he had a copy of *Playgirl* magazine in his pocket," said Chris.

"I don't think that had anything to do with their attitude," put in Phemeral. "The man saw one in my briefcase, too, but he couldn't possibly be that bigoted. As a matter of fact, *Playgirl* has special rates for clergymen. I get a lot of raw material out of it for my ethical studies."

"That registers," said Chris.

Hooper now addressed Densely. "Maybe we can be of some help, as you suggested. Didn't you say that you were a believer?"

"Of course I am."

"And that you are now trusting in Christ?"

"Absolutely."

"I don't mean to be intrusive, but let me just ask one more question. How is it that you trust in Christ, brother?"

"Well, if you want to get technical, I believe that Christ graciously accepts my obedience to him."

"He does what?" asked Chris, his jaw dropping.

"I mean he makes my conduct as a Christian and my life of service to humanity acceptable, so that I stand justified before God."

"Did you tell that to the man at the gate?"

"I did. I also told him I was a church member in very good standing, which I am. Matter of fact I've been a board member for years, and what's more, a heavy contributor."

"What did he say?"

"He wanted to know where I got my ideas about Christ and on what authority I based them. He was a foreigner, this man—I think he said he was a Malay from Singapore. Anyway, I told him my authority was the simple testimony of my own dedicated heart, and if that wasn't a Christian statement I don't know what is. But for some reason or other neither he nor the man he referred me to seemed to think it was sufficient."

"What about you, Dr. Phemeral?" asked Hooper.

"Why, it was quite humiliating, actually. I was turned over to a couple of counselors and oddly enough, they were from out of the country, too. One was from Ceylon, I believe, and one from somewhere in East Africa. Of course you understand I consider myself a world citizen and completely without prejudice; but they got me involved in a discussion about the difference between correct behavior caused by external pressures and good behavior caused by a change of will. This happens to be my field and I know ten times more about it than they do, but there was no use arguing with them. I didn't come up with the right clichés so they rejected me. They asked me about my church, too. That seemed a bit odd. I knew they had missions in Ceylon, but I wasn't aware that they had churches. I had to tell them frankly that I gave up preaching years ago and haven't been attending church in some time. But I can't see why that would keep me from doing some research inside the city. After all, I'm not going in there to corrupt anybody. I'd like to use their libraries and facilities for a couple of weeks and do a little inquiring. This kind of inquisition troubles me. It seems to come right out of the Dark Ages."

"I've been wondering while you were speaking," said Manly, "if the word 'repentance' was mentioned to either one of you."

"Of course," snapped Phemeral. "That was precisely the issue. They tried to tell me it was the changed will that indicated true repentance. I told them such terms may sound impressive in a theological textbook in their part of the world, but I had some case histories in my briefcase in which the motives were so mixed that you couldn't tell whether it was the will or the heart or the mind or the glands or the hormones that determined the behavior."

"But you do think a man needs to repent, don't you?" asked Chris. "Of his wrongdoings, I mean."

"Not necessarily," replied the doctor. "I don't expect you to be familiar with the latest hermeneutical interpretations, but let me try to summarize. Theologians now consider that all this talk about sinners needing to be converted is not only psychologically unsound, it's completely unbiblical."

"How could it be unbiblical, when Jesus said, 'Except ye repent, ye shall all likewise perish'?" asked Hooper.

"Proof texts mean nothing," announced Phemeral. "They only betray an ignorance of the real teaching of the New Testament, which is that Christ died for all men, therefore all men are restored in him. That is, all men are saved. They are in the Kingdom right now, and they are no more in need of repentance and conversion than are the fish in that fountain."

"I don't get it," said Chris.

"Let me put it in Biblical terminology," continued the doctor. " 'God was in Christ reconciling the world to himself.' That means the world is now his. That's all there is to it. What we ought to do is start celebrating!"

Hooper turned to the doctor's companion. "Did you get into this?" he asked.

"Not exactly. I got stuck with some odd types too. They must be short of help around here. This Malaysian at the gate referred me to a swarthy fellow who said he was from Argentina. He wanted to know if I stood before God with confidence. Can you imagine that?"

"What did you tell him?"

"I said of course I did; if a man doesn't have some kind of confidence in himself, he isn't worth a nickel. Then we got into a hassle about the Bible. He asked if I accepted the authority of the Word of God, and I told him frankly that I did, but I also accepted the consensus of scholarly opinion. I said I wasn't about to throw out the assured results of scientific investigations of Scripture. He didn't seem to like that. He didn't think the assured results were all that sure, he said. He wanted to know if I could make a more positive statement. I was forced to tell him I thought his brains were a little scrambled. So we got nowhere."

"I'm sorry about this," said Manly. "I would like to help you fellows, but I don't know where to begin. Maybe Mr. Anders does."

"Why don't we tell them what the Lord did for us?" suggested Chris.

"Go ahead."

Chris stood up and put his hands on his hips. "Well, I

just got to the end of my rope in Doomsdale, and set out looking for God. I didn't really know what I was doing, but I guess the Lord did. Anyway, I went through this transmitter and learned some things about the meaning of faith. Then I went up a hill they called Gordon's Calvary and asked to be forgiven and I put my life in the hands of Christ. Something happened. I can't explain it, but I knew I was born again. So then they gave me a Bible and told me to start traveling, and here I am."

"I did the same thing, pretty much," added Hooper, "except I'm ashamed to say I fell by the wayside and spent two whole years working for the devil. But now I'm back, and I can tell you it's for keeps. If you would want to—"

"Your stories are very nice," interrupted Phemeral, "but they are a trifle naïve, and I'm afraid they're not going to help us much in our present situation."

"I agree," said Chris abruptly. "As far as I'm concerned, you've had it."

"What makes you say that?" demanded Densely.

"Are you sure you want to know? It's because this is no place for you. There are no tourist traps inside that gate. You'd be bored to death in Life City, if it's what I think it is."

"Why not let me be the judge of that?"

"Well, I don't make the rules about who gets in and who doesn't, but I can tell you there's something fishy about some of your ideas."

"Fishy? In what way?" persisted Densely, now highly indignant.

"Why, your scheme has got Christ justifying not your person, but your actions. He never said he'd do that, so far as I know. I'm not walking through that gate on the red carpet of my good deeds, Mr. Densely, and I'm not crawling in on the broken glass of my remorse. I'm going in on the grace of God, because I'm a sinner and because that's the only way I'll get there. But you never once mentioned your sins. I don't believe you think you're lost or that you deserve hell. You think God loves you because you're so good to him."

"You're entitled to your opinion. Actually it works both ways. He's good to me and I'm good to him."

"But what it comes down to is, you're being good to yourself. As for your doctor friend, I daresay he knows a whole lot but he can't seem to sort it out. He says Christ died for everybody, so everybody's going to glory. But if I was saved back in Doomsdale, how come I left home? How come everything in my life fell apart? You fellows ought to be honest enough to admit the truth: you've worked out a cheap plastic imitation of salvation. You think you can have all this and Life City too; that you can come to Jesus without going down on your knees; that you can love your neighbor and your neighbor's wife at the same time."

"Oh, I wouldn't carry situation ethics quite that far, I don't believe," said Phemeral, beginning to smile.

"Wouldn't you, now?" said Chris, turning to him. "Let me say something about your ethics. You and the computers are trying to decide what makes men act right, but you're overlooking the clearest thing ever written on the subject, and that's the Bible. I found myself in the Bible, Doctor, and I found you too. And I can tell you that's the place to start if you're making a study of human behavior. Otherwise you're wasting your time, whether you do research in Life City or any place else."

"Here's another type with brain fever, Doctor," said Densely to Phemeral. "Must be an epidemic in these parts."

"He's right about one thing," replied Phemeral. "We're wasting our time." He stood up and reached for his brief-case.

"Wait," said Chris. He walked over to Densely, who had also got to his feet. Putting his hand on the man's shoulder, Chris said, "I'm a young Christian with a lot to learn. I didn't mean to offend you—or the doctor—with sharp words. Will you take my apology?"

"There's nothing to apologize for," said Densely. "Religion does different things to different people."

Chris took a memory verse packet out of his pocket. "Then will you take this as a present from me?"

"What is it?"

"Just some verses."

"Really!" said Phemeral impatiently.

"It definitely would help your ethical research," said Manly, turning to him, "if you took a look at Paul's letters."

"I'll make a note of it," said Phemeral, nodding as he walked toward his car. Awkwardly, Densely took the packet, stuffed it in his pocket and hurried after him.

Chapter 16

THE travelers were now free at last to complete the final few yards of their journey. A strange exhilaration swept over Chris as they strolled across the tiled plaza to the portal of the city, Bibles in hand. "I feel," he said, "as if I have never done a single worthwhile thing in my whole life, and yet here I am about to be honored and treated like royalty."

"The way you put it to them is true," said Manly. "It's God's grace. Grace got us out of DeSpare and grace brought us here, and when we go through it'll be just more grace."

The treatment was indeed royal so far as courtesy and graciousness went, but the process at the gate was more complicated than they had expected. The first man on duty, whom Chris guessed to be a Mexican, sat behind a high desk and asked to see their Bibles. He examined them briefly, smiled and returned them. The next official had the blue eyes of an Icelander. He switched on an amber light that was beamed into their faces and scrutinized their foreheads as Captain

Petrovich had done, explaining, "This is a routine check of the mark that was stamped on you back there on the hill."

"I remember it," said Chris, "but I thought it rubbed off long ago."

"It never wears off," said the man, smiling and waving them on.

At the next booth they were asked by a man with a Canadian maple leaf in his buttonhole if they had anything to declare. They took out the cards that had been given them by van Gelst just before leaving the Delectable Mountains.

"I declare," said Manly, reading his card, "the Gospel: that Christ died for our sins according to the Scriptures; that he was buried; and that he rose again the third day according to the Scriptures."

"I declare," said Chris in turn, "that God is light, and in him is no darkness at all. If we walk in the light, as he is in the light, we have fellowship one with another, and the blood of Jesus his Son cleanses us from all sin."

"Is this your sworn personal testimony, and do you have anything else to declare?" asked the Canadian.

"That's it," they both replied.

"Very well, gentlemen," he said cordially. "Proceed to the next booth where you will check in your wallets and watches. You won't be needing them while you are staying here."

Farther along a young lady who said she was from Samoa fitted each of them with a special pair of sunglasses. "It takes a few days to get used to the lighting in our city," she explained, "but you'll learn to love it." Then an affable Dutchman provided them with gilt-dipped sandals, and they were issued complete linen outfits, including Bermuda shorts, by an Eskimo from St. Lawrence Island. Somewhere along the line a hymnbook was added to the pile.

After they had finished the processing they came to a limousine awaiting them at the curb inside the gate. The words *Paradise Inn* were lettered on its door. "Your accommodations have all been arranged, and a special welcome is awaiting you," explained the young driver in a broad Australian accent. "Would you like to go to the inn now, or would you rather do a bit of sightseeing?"

"I'd like a nice long nap," said Manly. "I believe I'll go to the inn."

"So will I," said Chris, "but there's one place I'd like to visit first, if you don't mind."

The driver motioned to another limousine parked behind him. "That will be no problem, gentlemen," he said. "This car will take Mr. Hooper to his lodgings, and I will drive Mr. Anders wherever he wishes to go."

The friends parted and Chris got into the first limousine. "Would you please take me down to the bank of the river?" he asked.

"With pleasure." They drove along a broad thoroughfare whose dazzling appearance was not clearly evident to Chris, due to the special glasses he was wearing. What he could make out of the scenery seemed to him a perfect harmonizing of natural landscape with planting and architecture. Memories of his arduous journey lingered in his mind, as aches and pains continued to rack his body, so that he felt himself in a kind of daze. Much as his body hurt from the jail beating, he knew it would soon be well. His ankle already felt a great deal better. But there were other hurts—spiritual failures and thoughts of his family—which he doubted would heal so easily. Still, through it all he felt himself enfolded by a strange peace.

"Will we be given an audience before the King, do you suppose?" he asked the driver.

The man turned and looked at him. "That's a hard one to answer, mate," he responded. Then he added, "Don't you remember me?"

"I'm terrible about faces," apologized Chris, "but you do look—you're not—"

"Philip! I was at the transmitter. I helped you get started for Gordon's Calvary."

"Of course. So now you're back here?"

"Right. Wherever there's help needed, that's where I aim to be."

"Is it nice here?" asked Chris timidly.

"I love it. You will too. Here we are at the riverbank, sir. Watch your step." The limousine pulled into a turnout from which a series of steps led down a grassy bank to the edge of the wide stream. It was a good half-mile across to the other side, as nearly as Chris could judge.

"No bridges, I take it?"

"No bridges, no pontoons, no hydrofoils, no ferry boats."

"Could you wait here ten minutes for me?"

"Take your time."

Chris walked slowly down the bank until he stood on its lip, looking into the limpid, gently flowing water. He took off his sunglasses and stared across the blue expanse, trying to make out some features on the other side. He thought he could see some moving figures in white, but could not be sure. His eyes were not much good at distances. All at once he cocked an ear; faintly over the water came the sound of

music. It seemed to be a hymn they were singing. He thought
he recognized it, but couldn't tell which one it was. The words
were indistinguishable, yet he remembered the line in the
tune that went, "My chains fell off, my heart was free, I—
something—went forth, and—something—thee."

Well Rusty if that's you singing over there I just wish I
were with you If only I had brought some field glasses I swear
I see someone waving Oh God I feel sick I want to be with
You I want to be with Rusty It's nice here but everything
seems so flat and stale compared with joining You over there
Why couldn't they have taken me in that copter too Why
did they just take Rusty All I got by staying on this side was
a clobbering within an inch of my life God I'm so homesick
for Heaven I can't stand it I want to see Jesus I want to go
home where I came from I want to be rid of my sins forever
and stand and gaze at your glory Sorry if I'm bawling but God
this is the closest I've ever been to the heavenlies and it's
just so wonderful I don't ever want to leave here except to
go over there Send that copter Lord and tell those hikers I'm
ready . . . .

"I'm sorry, sir, but a radio call has come in for me," Philip
said gently. "May I help you up? That does it. I'll take you
right over to Paradise Inn now."

Chris sat in the back seat wiping his eyes with his handker-
chief. "Thanks for indulging me," he said. "It was something
I had looked forward to for a long time."

"Good on you!" said Philip. "I've got a few buddies over
there myself. It's nice knowing they're so close by."

"It really is the same city, isn't it?" asked Chris.

"That's right. And we're all citizens and subjects of the

same King. You might say it's the church militant on one side and the church triumphant on the other."

"What do I do tomorrow, do you know?"

"Yes sir. Tomorrow is the Lord's Day. We praise God together and then we take it easy. Sound good?"

"It certainly does. Do we all go to the same house of worship?"

"It's this way, mate. We go to the place that's most congenial to us. Some of us like to stand, some to sit, and some to kneel. But it's all the same Gospel and the same Lord."

"Then what do we do?"

Philip pointed to a rounded structure of delicate design they were just passing. "There's your induction center," he said. "You'll be starting a series of training programs in there Monday that'll fit you right for the King's service. It's a marvelous course, really."

"How long does it last?"

"We never finish—not until the Great Reassignment! They just keep sending us out in teams now and then on special missions. We go all over the world, you know. I wonder if you remember Colonel Goodall."

"Yes, very well."

"He'll be your instructor at the beginning."

"I think I'm going to like it. Where do you suppose they'll send me first?"

"You're married, aren't you, sir?"

"I sure am. Four children, all boys, and a wife living in Doomsdale."

"Ah well, there's not much doubt about where you'll be sent."

"You mean I'll be commissioned to get them and bring them to Life City?"

Philip did not answer. Instead he drove into the very handsome grounds of a resort hotel modeled after a South Sea village. Coconut palms—were they coconut?—lined the driveway. Tiny cottages with rounded thatched roofs were attractively strung along the sandy shore of a lake. Tropical flowers bloomed in abundance, and birds of dazzling color chattered from huge banyan trees. Green hills rose in the distance.

Philip jumped out and opened the door for Chris. "Here you are, Mr. Anders," he said. "Paradise Inn, the best of both worlds. Some of your friends will be joining you this evening for dinner. It's been nice seeing you again, sir."

Chris got out, looked around, blinked, swallowed, and held out his hand to the young Australian. "God in your heart, Philip," he said.

Chapter 17

"CHRIS," called Eileen up the narrow stairs. "Are you coming down to breakfast, or shall I throw out the rest of this batter?"

OK praise God I'll take a thatched cottage by the lake if one's available I'll need a key I said I'll need a key to stir up this batter Ugh Who wants breakfast after My mouth tastes like the inside of a cameldriver's mitt Hey that's pretty funny What time is it I wonder if it was the pillow on my face when I thought Belial had his forearm up against my throat Didn't I go on that trip Didn't I get stuck in that creek or fight off those birds or spend two days in prison Didn't that jailer batter me with his hose Batter stir the batter Eileen Boy is my mouth dry Batter bought a bit of butter I did talk to You God didn't I You did stamp my forehead and say I belonged to You didn't You But what about Rusty and those whiskey bottles Did I almost die Is that why I dreamt about the helicopter I don't have the key It was in my wallet Oh good grief here I am back in the old home town No Paradise Inn

No sandy beach in the sun Just a list of Sunday customer calls to make and. . . .

"Chris! Did you hear me?"

"Yaaaah. Aaaaah. I'm comin'."

"Will you drive us to Sunday School, Dad?" asked Jeffrey. "The teacher's taking us on a hike up Big Top afterward."

"Huh?" Chris stood by the kitchen table, blinking watery eyes—he held a coffee cup in a trembling hand and stared distractedly at the waffle iron, then at his son. "What's all that racket out there?"

"Oh, just starlings," said Eileen. "They'll go away. Will you take the boys or won't you?"

"Starlings!" Chris shuffled to the window and looked out, rubbing his head with his free hand. His gaze fell upon his oldest son opening the garage door. "Now what's he doing with that Mustang?"

"He's washing it," barked Dean. "What do you think he's doing? You told him to."

Chris ignored him and turned to Eileen. "You wanta go?" he asked.

"I've got a roast to put in. Some man called you over an hour ago. Woke me up."

"Who was it?"

"I don't remember. Hess or Ness or something like that."

Chris' eyes opened wide. "You're kidding," he said.

"Dad," said Dana.

"What's the matter with you?" demanded Eileen. "Why don't you stop stumbling around and sit down and eat your breakfast?"

"Was it Rusty Ness?"

"How should I know who it was? His number's on the pad over there."

Chris sat down. "All right, pipe down everybody," he announced. "Was this food ever prayed over?" There was silence in the room. "Then let's bow our heads. Heavenly Father, we ask a blessing on this manna—this food, and give us grace, and, uh, oh, in Jesus' name, Amen. More coffee, please!"

"Dad," said Dana.

"I think Dad's been on a trip," said Dean. "I bet Mom put some LSD in his coffee."

"I'll LSD you," mumbled Chris between mouthfuls of waffle.

Jerry came in the kitchen door for some hot water. "Hi, Pa," he said. "You got some new dents in your chassis."

"Humph," said Chris.

"Dad," said Jeffrey.

"See the picture of our new coach in the Sunday paper?" Jerry asked. Chris shook his head. "Look!" Jerry put the sports page in front of his father, and there was the erstwhile bulldozer operator himself, ugly face and all, staring at him. Chris looked at the masthead (*Dimsdale Times* it read) and the name in the cutline ("Coach B. E. Lisle") and promptly spilled coffee on his pajamas.

"Will you take that paper away?" he asked testily. "This stuff burns, you know." As Jerry removed the offending pages Chris noticed the front headline, ASIA CRISIS BREWING.

"Will you take us to Sunday School, Dad?" asked Dana.

"OK, OK, now leave me alone, will you? I've got to think." He reflected a moment, then called the two smaller boys back. "Here, I've got something for you." He gave them a squeeze and a kiss. "You're all sticking with me, understand?"

Fifteen minutes later, after placing the telephone call, Chris summoned the family once again to the kitchen where Eileen was washing the dishes. "Here's what's up," he said. "A friend of mine has invited us to some special meetings at Lakeview Church, and I want us all to go tonight. If they like, the boys can ride with Jerry."

"Not with me," said Jerry. "I'm surfing till dark."

"We won't get back from Big Top in time," said Jeffrey. "It's a long ways."

"There's something on at the city park," said Dean.

"All right," replied Chris, "I'll put it to you. If you want to eat this week, be here at seven o'clock."

"But, Dad," said Dean. Dana started to cry. Chris walked out of the kitchen, went upstairs and prepared to shave. He glanced out the bathroom window and watched Jerry move the Mustang to let another car through the alley. He noted that the driver was an older person; then he looked again. The man smiled and waved as he passed Jerry. No doubt about it; it was Guy Wise, or his double. Chris returned to his shaving with a hand that trembled slightly. After his shower he came into the bedroom to find Eileen tidying the dresser.

"Why did you spring this on the boys all of a sudden?" she asked.

"I don't know," he said. "Maybe because someone just sprang it on me."

"Who is this person?"

"Oh, he's a fellow who used to sell computers for a competitor. I knew him."

"What's he doing now?"

"He's in some kind of church work. Told me about this

fellow that's preaching tonight at Lakeview and I said sure I'd come. I know the guy; he's great."

"Where did you run into him? I see by the paper he's a Frenchman."

"Well, I met him at a barbecue."

Eileen straightened up from her bedmaking. "When did you ever go to a barbecue?"

Chris ran a hand through his hair. "I just ask you to come and bring the boys as a favor to me," he said.

At a quarter to seven that night the Anders family went through another crisis. "Where's my passport?" Chris demanded in tones not particularly gentle.

"Your what?" echoed Eileen.

"My pass—my Bible. Where's my Bible? Somebody's taken it out of the bookcase." One after another denied knowledge of its disappearance until Jerry came in the front door at one minute to seven.

"Marcia borrowed it over the weekend," Jerry admitted. "She had to write a theme and I knew you never used it. How come it's suddenly a top-priority item?"

"I was reading it just last week," Chris said. "And who is Marcia?"

"She's the new girl across the street."

"Would you kindly retrieve it from Marcia so I can take it to church?"

Five minutes later a bouncy, smiling teen-ager with long yellow hair came to the front door, Bible in hand. Chris answered the bell and found himself staring at her rather unduly. "You're Marcia?" he inquired.

"That's me!" She handed him the Bible, and he came to himself and thanked her. As she turned he stopped her.

"Mind if I ask you a question?"

"Not at all."

"What's your middle name?"

"Don't have one."

"No other name?"

"No." She laughed embarrassedly. "I did have one but I dropped it a long time ago. It was awful—kind of a family thing they'd kept going for generations. You see, our people came from New England."

"I can tell you what it was," said Chris with a grin.

Marcia frowned and looked a bit frightened. "What?"

"Discretion."

Marcia gasped, turned and ran across the street.

The rest of the evening seemed to Chris almost as much a dream as had the long sleep of the night before. The Anders family showed up late at the church and promptly got into an argument because all four boys wanted to sit in the balcony. Chris and Eileen finally agreed to accompany them upstairs. They were escorted by an usher who, if he were not Mr. Upman the roadworker, certainly looked like him. Chris had some difficulty seeing clearly in the church, as the lighting was not too effective and the distance to the pulpit was considerable. Nevertheless it seemed to him that the men's trio that sang bore a marked resemblance to the three hikers he had seen on Gordon's Calvary. Moreover, the man who made the announcements and took the offering—evidently the minister of the church—reminded him strangely of Ernie van Gelst.

The speaker of the evening was, as Rusty Ness had promised, none other than Mr. André LaBourd. Instead of being a shepherd from the Delectable Mountains, he was an international conference speaker known as the "Basque Bible Teacher." The church bulletin stated that he was conducting a one-week "deeper life mission" at the Lakeview Church in which other churches were cooperating. Mr. LaBourd, it said, was the founder of a prayer fellowship that kept him traveling around the world on Bible study missions. Next week he would be in Cassopolis; his colleague, Mr. Ness, was there already, helping to organize prayer groups in the churches.

Memories of the barbecue Gospel meeting kept flooding into Chris' mind as he studied the lean, brown face that broke into wrinkles with every smile. What a personality! And what a message! LaBourd had chosen for his text the Twenty-third Psalm. Simplicity and rugged honesty marked his presentation.

"What are you looking for?" he asked. "So many people in evangelical churches today are looking for a brush fire, a big revival, no? But perhaps God's idea of *la gloire*—the glory—is different from ours. Perhaps Jesus did not raise the storms so much as quiet them down, I think. So our business is not so much to see revival as to be one of those being revived. Sometimes we can pray too much. Sometimes people don't want your prayers for revival, they want your testimony of revival.

"I would suggest that we do not talk so much about renewal or revival or spiritual awakening as we talk about Jesus. He is renewal. He is revival. He is spiritual awakening. There is no need to look for something beyond the Lord Jesus Christ, any more than there was need for Jean-Baptiste to ask, 'Are you the Coming One or should we look for another?' Instead of looking for an extra-special gift of the Spirit at this meeting, just come back to Calvary. If you received Jesus

Christ on that mountain, you have all the power you need. *Comprenez-vous?* We do not receive things by prayer, we receive them by Jesus.

"Perhaps you came here tonight to pull up your spiritual socks, eh? Perhaps you came to get what you call 'lifted up,' but I tell you it is Jesus who needs to be 'lifted up.' You want a big testimony to give your friends? I will give it to you: Just stop testifying to yourself. Stop giving out eloquence about being a stand-up Christian, and make a sinner's testimony. You think your Christian service is an answer to 'Christian' sin, *n'est-ce pas?* It is not. It is a substitute. *Vraiment!* It is a polite substitute. Come back to the cross and learn to be dust, and let God breathe into you the breath of life. Let him lead you out of the valley of the shadow into the house of the Lord."

Was this really the man whom Chris had heard in his dream, when he knew him as the shepherd of the Delectable Mountains? The accent was the same. Could it be a case of extrasensory perception? But he had other things to think about and did not try to speculate further.

God I wish I knew what You were up to tonight What my friend up there is saying is so true I know it's the answer to life He's getting through to me but Lord why did it seem so much more real in the dream Tearing through Beelzebul's Principality in that Mustang I felt like a hero but just sitting here flapping my ears at a preacher is so tame I'm trying to think of those verses You taught me that set fire to the car radio and opened the jail door I know now You've got the power that a man can live by Jesus I know about the blood I know You're coming back and taking over soon I know You brought me into Life City and wouldn't let me stay there

*but sent me back to get my family OK here they are Lord
but I can't do any more It's up to You now to draw them into
Your Kingdom I'll try to set an example but it's going to take
more than that What about Eileen How do you make a wife
understand what's happened to you Sure I know pray pray
pray Well shoot I am praying but speak to me God I'm going
to make all kinds of bloopers and boners in the Christian life
I need help bad Maybe if I maybe if I Now he's coming to the
close If he gives an invitation to come to Christ maybe if I go
up the others will come too Maybe they won't Maybe if they
do go up it won't mean a thing in the world but God I've got
to do something after what You did for me. . . .*

Gently the Bible teacher brought his message to a conclusion. Were there any who would like to come forward in dedication of heart and life to Jesus Christ? Any who wanted to make a fresh start? He was not, he pointed out, an evangelist; he thought of himself more as a pastor of souls, a shepherd. Yet the Holy Spirit had been speaking to him in an unusual way during the past few moments, and he felt constrained to ask if someone—perhaps someone upstairs there in the balcony. . . .

Chris pressed Eileen's hand, stood up and stepped out into the aisle.

Historical Note

Listed below are some of the distinctive characters and geographical place names of that seventeenth-century literary classic and allegory of the Christian life, *The Pilgrim's Progress,* by John Bunyan, with their counterparts in the present tale:

Persons

Christian	Christian Anders
	(Anders signifies *man*)
Christiana	Eileen
Matthew	Jerry
Samuel	Dean
Joseph	Jeffrey
James	Dana
Evangelist	Ernie van Gelst
Obstinate	O. B. Stennett
Pliable	Warren Clay
Helpful	Upman
Worldly Wiseman	Guy Wise
Legality	Doctor Liegel

Goodwill .... Colonel Goodall
Interpreter .... Major N. T. R. Putter
Man in the Iron Cage .... Man in Château d'If
The Shining Ones .... The Three Hikers
Simple, Sloth and Presumption ...... The Lazy 3
Formalist .... Seminarian in tuxedo
Hypocrisy .... Hippie
Timorous .... Tim O'Rowse
Little-faith .... Uncle Al
Faint-heart .... The Nephew
Watchful the Porter .... Captain Petrovich
Charity .... Char
Piety .... Patty
Prudence .... Pru
Discretion .... Creshie
Apollyon .... Belial
Faithful .... T. (Rusty) Ness
Talkative .... L. O. Quacious
Hopeful .... Manly Hooper
Lord Hate-good .... Max Spirochete
Mr. Blind-man .... General Pitt
A Shepherd .... André LaBourd
Giant Despair .... Judge Korah T. Failing
Temporary .... Dr. Freddie Phemeral
Ignorant .... John Densely

Places

City of Destruction .... Doomsdale
Slough of Despond .... Stuck Creek
Town of Morality .... Upper Striving
Town of Carnal Policy .... Carnapolis
The Wicket Gate and Shining Light .. The transmitter

Interpreter's House .... Major Putter's staff room
Hill Difficulty .... Poopout Hill
House Beautiful .... Pilgrims' Manor House
Valley of Humiliation .... Prone Valley
City of Vanity .... Pridesburg
Vanity Fair .... Abaddonland
Doubting Castle .... Township of DeSpare
The Celestial City, Mount Zion ...... Life City

69 70 71 72 73 10 9 8 7 6 5 4 3 2 1

161 " to program a *curing* accuracy of the grants"

186 you think you can buo you rights .·. wip at same tim"
hc — re do rihg ace to you latn
no upentar

176 Rev 21:16 Fall